LION'S QUEST

A LION'S PRIDE #12

EVE LANGLAIS

Copyright © 2020/2021 Eve Langlais

Cover Art by Yocla Designs © 2020/2021

Produced in Canada

Published by Eve Langlais

http://www.EveLanglais.com

E-ISBN: 978 1 77 384 190 8
Print ISBN: 978 1 77 384 191 5

All Rights Reserved

This book is a work of fiction and the characters, events and dialogue found within the story are of the author's imagination and are not to be construed as real. Any resemblance to actual events or persons, either living or deceased, is completely coincidental.

No part of this book may be reproduced or shared in any form or by any means, electronic or mechanical, including but not limited to digital copying, file sharing, audio recording, email and printing without permission in writing from the author.

PROLOGUE

Peter crept from the guest bed he'd scammed for the night.

Yes, scammed. As part of his plan, he'd ensured his car had broken down outside the door of an old house in Suzdal, Russia. He'd only briefly glanced at the architecture, still gorgeous despite the shabby exterior. Peeling paint, the paneling a fading gray, with the wood rotting in some places. Pity. It was probably a showpiece in its day.

The lady who answered the door appeared younger than expected for a woman approaching eighty. Visible still amidst the few wrinkles was beauty in the fine parchment skin, a long neck, and pure white hair pinned atop her head, a few tendrils curling loose. She wore a white blouse buttoned to her neck and a long, navy-hued skirt.

She greeted him in Russian, her voice holding a slight quaver as she asked him who he was.

"I'm Peter." He kept his last name to himself.

A torrent of Russian followed. Since his understanding of the language didn't go much further than asking for booze or food, he spoke in English. "Please. Can you help me? I have a flat tire." He gestured to his vehicle pulled over the curb. The front wheel was visibly in need of major aid on account he'd nailed a screw into it, pulled it back and forth a few times, then driven on it until it got the point.

The old lady eyed him, his car, and then said in very accented English, "You need a tire. We will call the garage. Come inside." She welcomed him into her home, hands spatting him over, as if she had to touch him. She offered him a bright smile with many white teeth and said, "I am Irina. Irina Koznetsov."

He almost thanked her for confirming it. He'd only gotten the briefest of information before coming to Irina's house. "Hi, Irina." He held her hand and smiled. "Thank you for your hospitality."

She patted his hand. "Thank you. I don't get to enjoy American boys often."

The odd phrasing threw him, but he chalked it up to a language thing. "Are you married?" he asked.

Irina tittered. "Was. They're dead."

"Meaning you're swinging and single." He winked, knowing how to pour on the charm.

The old lady grinned even wider. Fuck, she had some big teeth.

"You have girlfriend?" she asked.

"Haven't been lucky enough to find the one yet." He waxed eloquent, and Irina ate it up.

She fetched him some cookies and then what he thought was coffee with a bite. Too strong for what he wanted to do.

When she left for a minute, he poured some out.

Irina returned, carrying more food. Pure sugar decadence on a plate. As he orgasmed through whatever the fuck magic she put in it, Irina chattered some more. Told him she had a few children but the only family she saw regularly was her granddaughter, Svetlana.

Single granddaughter.

"I really should be calling the garage," he said before she tried to talk him into a date with Svetlana.

"The car is already gone." Irina waved her hand. "I call my friend.

Well, that put a crimp in his plan. "Gone where?"

"To the garage. He fix it. You get in the morning."

"Morning. Wow." He scrubbed a hand through his hair. "I don't suppose you know of a hotel nearby?"

"No."

"No worries. I'll find one." He went to leave, but Irina stopped him.

"You stay. I have bed," she offered.

"I wouldn't want to impose."

"Stay. Stay. Drink. Eat." She pushed food and that noxious liquid at him.

He couldn't drink it, so he kept dumping it. Hopefully she wouldn't notice the wet spot he was creating as it poured it in between the couch cushions.

He fake-yawned before she could give him another glass.

"Bedtime!" she announced, clapping her hands. "Follow." She went toward the kitchen rather than the second floor where he knew the bedrooms were.

Was there a second staircase?

His phone beeped. He pulled it out to see yet another text from his sister, checking on him. He'd reply when he had time. He had the phone in hand when he entered the kitchen.

Irina stood by a door with stairs going down. "You follow," she said then frowned. "Who you call?"

He waggled the phone. "It's my sister. She keeps track of me."

"She know you here?"

There was something in the way she said that raised the hair on his neck. It gave him the chills. Which was crazy. As if she could hurt him. Still...

"Yeah, my sister and I are close. She knows everything that happens to me. We talk all the time." Not entirely true. She clung. He strove for space.

The old lady muttered something before shutting the door. She moved past him back out of the kitchen.

"Um, Irina?"

"Bedtime. You tired."

"Yes, tired." He was also confused but happy to see them going upstairs instead of down into the basement. Never liked those. Hadn't for a long time. Cold. Dank. Musty, nasty places.

Irina showed him to a room, masculine in feel with dark furniture and fabrics. She shut the door, still muttering, and he almost fist-pumped. He was in.

So easy. A different man might have felt bad about conning an old lady.

He was not that man. He paced as he waited. Almost nine o'clock. When would she go to sleep?

He heard the most subtle of creaks and moved to the door. Pressed his ear on it. Could have sworn he heard heavy breathing. The skin on his body pimpled.

Then came steps as if someone walked away.

It was then he realized he held his breath. Now, it was just after midnight—more than two hours since he'd last heard a creak—when he emerged from under the sheets, fully dressed. He'd scouted where he needed to go early on in the evening, after the call to the garage but before she brought out like the seventh dessert. All he'd had to say was, "This house is magnificent. I don't suppose you could give me the tour and history?"

With obvious pride, Irina showed off her home, painting a picture that helped him see past the cracks in the plaster, the worn floors, and the dust in the corners. The grandeur still peeked from rooms with mismatched pieces.

It was Irina who pointed to a clean spot on the floor. "I own big—big—*klavesin*." She resorted to Russian.

He didn't know the word but could guess given the bench with music sheets on it left behind. A piano or harpsichord, he 'd guess. "What happened to it?"

"Sold to fix roof." She glared at the ceiling.

He could only hope she'd not sold what he'd come looking for.

But he feared for nothing. He saw the key the moment she opened the door on the second floor to her sewing room, packed into a turret, with a comfortable rocking chair by the window, a basket of yarn beside it. A sewing machine, almost buried by bolts of fabric, some of it sun faded and dusty, sat under a window. The wrought iron key hung from an obviously handmade chandelier, the key just one of many mismatched items dangling, like the ornate fork and an etched goblet.

"What an interesting piece of art."

She saw him looking. "It's garbage."

Had she ever heard the adage one person's junk was another's treasure?

"This is the kind of thing my sister would love. I don't suppose you'd sell it?" Peter tried to do it the right way. The honest way.

"No." Irina shook her head. "Babushka make me."

He could have pressed the point to see if that sentimentality had a price, but it was easier to creep from his bed after midnight to steal it. Irina would never notice one key gone from that monster lamp shade, but just in case, he'd brought a close replica. After all, the job came with sketches of what he was supposed to look for. If he swapped it right, no one would ever know the difference.

Did he have any qualms about stealing from the old lady? Not many. His sister thought he was a good guy. And he was. For her.

But this key was special. It could set him up for life, and when that happened, he'd make sure Irina got a portion of it. Maybe he'd have her house fixed. Hire her some help. Get a shrink to absolve him and blame his actions on his childhood.

The good deeds he could do with that key justified

his entering the sewing room. Reaching on tiptoe, he could grasp the key, but unhooking it proved impossible. He needed a few more inches. He eyed the footstool, but the spindly legs were for resting feet not the full weight of a man.

The sewing machine table appeared heavy, leaving him only one choice. He moved the rocking chair and, with careful maneuvering that included him hovering in a squat, ended up on the seat.

It wobbled, and he held out his arms to balance then straightened fully so that he could manipulate the wire holding the key in place. It truly was a testament to recycling. The metal rim was made of old coat hangers bent and twisted into a frame from which dangled the oddest collection of stuff on metal filament.

The key wasn't the only thing that caught his eye. As he happened to glance out the window, he could have sworn he saw the brief flicker as of someone lighting a cigarette. Could be someone out for a walk.

Still, he shouldn't dawdle. His fingers protested the tough metal. The filament took some time to untangle, but he freed the heavier than expected key, the coldness of it sending a shiver through him.

He ignored a feeling of foreboding and put it into his pocket even as he wondered at his next move. Leave in the night or stay for breakfast?

Given the hearty dinner Irina fed him, he almost drooled as he wondered what he could expect for the first meal of the day. Surely better than he could get on the way back to the city.

His tummy decided it. He'd leave in the morning.

Now for the next step, a precaution if you will. Fake key to take its place. He'd actually had two fabricated. The second one was hidden in his apartment, ready to hand over to the people who hired him.

Don't feel bad. They weren't good people.

The fake key went up, a closer replica than expected given he'd had the 3D printer make it off images that didn't show all the parts. The new ornament looked seamless.

Before he could climb down from the rocking chair, he glanced out the window again. The cigarette smoker was gone. Just him and his trespasses out and about.

His bad luck too.

There was a reason he'd gone to prison in the past, because somehow, so many of his best-laid plans failed for stupid reasons. In this case? The rocking chair gave only a single warning creak before it collapsed. As in, splintered into pieces. He thudded to the floor.

There was nothing quiet about it. The grimace stayed on his face the entire time he stood silent in the debris, listening. He didn't hear the old lady coming to look, but she was sure to notice the next time she came into the sewing room. Staying the rest of the night suddenly didn't seem like the best option.

A sense of urgency filled him. He exited the sewing room and moved into the hall. His door was at the far end; however, the one to the old lady's suite was ajar. It had been closed when he came up the hall.

Oh shit. Was she up? Had she already called the cops? He couldn't tell if she was in her room or downstairs. Could be she went for a glass of warm milk. Personally, he'd never used that nasty white shit to help him sleep. Give him a joint any day.

Inanity helped him focus. Stealthy mice had nothing on him as he eased up the hall, darting into his room only long enough to grab his knapsack. It was when he was about to leave, he saw the tiger.

He blinked. Opened his eyes wide.

Still there.

Fuck me, a tiger.

Where had it come from? He'd not seen any signs Irina owned a pet.

"Grrr." The rumbling growl of warning didn't bode well, nor did the raised hackles on the feline's back.

Peter backed toward the window, a mental catalogue of the house reminding him of the peaked porch roof outside his room then a short drop to the ground.

But opening the window meant putting his back to a tiger.

Doing nothing got his face eaten.

He whirled and tugged. The old wooden pane didn't budge. Instinct more than anything had him throwing himself sideways. Just in time too!

The tiger soared past and hit the window hard then slumped to the floor, lying there, barely moving as if groggy.

He didn't waste that rare bit of good luck. He raced for the hall and down the stairs, no longer caring who he woke. Not with a tiger on the loose.

Out the door he went, and he was down two steps before it occurred to him to whirl and close it. After all, tigers couldn't open doors. But Irina could.

To his surprise, his car was parked in the driveway. The garage must have delivered it earlier than expected. His strides to reach it felt like a mile as he kept expecting something striped to pounce. He fumbled with his keys. Glass shattered, and a roar split the night.

Holy fuck. Peter slammed into his car and started it. The automated features turned on the headlights. He hit the brake and had shifted it into drive when he saw it.

Animal eyes with that weird glow reflected in the bright beams. The tiger stalked toward him, snarling.

Close enough he could see the gray in the fur. The stiffness of its pace.

An old tiger doing right by its owner.

Dammit. He'd always had a soft spot for big felines, which was why he didn't run it over but swerved and headed in the other direction.

He would later regret that choice.

CHAPTER ONE

"I need you to guard a human."

Nora eyed Arik, the lion king. "Am I in trouble for something? Being punished?" It might have emerged a tad sassier than was respectful because the job sounded like a demotion to her.

"On the contrary. This task could be the most important thing anyone can do right now."

She arched a brow. "Babysitting a human, important?" Unless this person was the president or something, she couldn't see it.

"Questioning me?" Arik said softly then stared at her, nothing more. He didn't have to do anything. As king of the Lion's Pride, East Coast division, his word was law.

It should be noted, he wouldn't harm her if she argued. She could say no and walk away, but the king would remember her disobedience, and her standing in the Pride would diminish. Not to mention, would Arik really ask her to watch over someone for no reason?

"Okay, who's the guy or gal?"

"Peter Montgomery. Lives alone. No partner or close friends, but he does have a sister."

"Am I restricting her access?"

Arik shook his head, his golden mane of hair perfectly layered and gorgeous. "No. But if you are around when she comes visiting, watch what you say."

"She doesn't know we're watching her brother?"

"Charlie, his sister, knows we're lending a hand. She's aware of the danger, and what we are, but her brother has no idea."

She frowned. "Charlie? Wait, you mean the human girl who married Lawrence?" Considered the most eligible bachelor, she'd had a few fantasies about the playkitty in her time. She'd skipped the wedding due to previous plans.

"That's the one. Peter is her brother, and he's oblivious about what we are." And it would stay that way unless there were extenuating circumstances. The circle of knowledge about their existence remained tight.

Double whammy. "In other words, I need to play him like I'm a dirty secret. Got it."

Arik coughed. "Yeah, I don't think you need to get

that close. Surveillance should be enough to start and protection in case someone comes after him."

Boring. "No problem. Where's he staying?" She really hoped they could shove him in a suite at the condo complex.

"One of our public Pride Group properties." The public ones being the buildings that housed humans, making their business portfolio appear more balanced to any observant types.

"If you're worried about his safety, it would be easier to guard him where we have lots of eyes." And by eyes she didn't just mean the security cameras. Shifters had keen hunter senses despite decades of city living. If someone tried anything on their turf, they'd know and act.

"I don't know if I want those chasing him getting that close to us."

"They're that dangerous?" she hotly exclaimed.

"I'm not exaggerating when I say what you're doing could be of utmost importance. Peter must be watched."

"I assume you've started surveillance?" Nora asked.

"While he was still on the honeymoon cruise with his sister, the Pride subtly arranged to have an apartment leased to him and fitted with security." Arik slid over a key. "You have a place in the building so you can be close by. This is an in-the-field op. You will have restricted contact with the Pride during it. If you need something, run it by me first."

"I'm gonna need tech probably." She knew right away she'd better mention it.

"Already good to go. Melly will work with you on anything you might need."

"What if I need backup?"

"Already in place. You'll split surveillance with Zachary Lennox."

Zachary was a solid bloke. She'd worked with him before.

"I don't care how you split the hours. Whatever works for you. I've already rented you both an apartment in the same building to make it easier. Your cover story will have you as living together, with Zach working from home as a software designer."

Which would allow them to bring in computer equipment without question. "What about me? What's my cover job story?"

"You are the new deli counter girl at the charcuterie across the street from the bookstore where Montgomery works."

She blinked. "You have me slinging meat?"

"Yes. It's the perfect spot to keep watch while he's at work."

"If you're not available, is there anyone else I can talk to if I hit a pinch?"

"Secrecy is important. No one but myself, the Omega, and the Beta." Only those in the highest echelon of the Pride would receive her reports. All requests for aid would have to go through the king or his seconds.

"You haven't said what I'm watching for."

"Because we're not one hundred percent sure what we're looking for. We do know it involves an old book, a key, and humans desperate to find some kind of treasure."

"Ooh. What kind of treasure?"

"The kind that might entail the destruction of our kind." An ominous declaration. "Which is why it's so important you find out what Peter knows."

She crinkled her nose. "You're not making sense. You said this Peter fellow doesn't know about shifters, so how could he pose a danger?"

"What if I told you there was a way to make you human, forever?"

She recoiled. "Ew. No."

"Right?"

Her jaw dropped. "Wait, you're serious."

"Very."

"But that's—"

"Impossible?" Arik eyed her intently, and she wilted.

"Fuck." Because if it existed, in the wrong hands, it could wipe them out.

"We've made attempts to extract anything he might know about the hidden treasure; however, he's claiming amnesia."

"Convenient."

"Isn't it though? Apparently, Mr. Peter Montgomery managed to get lost in the Russian wilderness for six months and, when he was finally found, claimed no memory of anything since he went missing."

"Six months in the wilds and lived? Bullshit." She snorted, mostly because she knew how unforgiving that landscape could be, having gone there on a class trip long ago. Nice country, though, if too many bears.

"There are many things about his story that don't ring true; however, to act against Peter would upset Lawrence's mate. Nor is it yet warranted. I'd rather try a more subtle approach first."

"By watching the human and waiting for him to slip up?"

"Yes."

"Sounds easy enough."

"Did I mention the part where we've already countered two attempts to apprehend Peter since he resurfaced?"

"They tried to kidnap, not kill?" she mused aloud. "Meaning someone is interested in what's inside his head."

"And they're working with humans," was his ominous reply. Left unsaid but implied: Their secret was at risk.

"How do we know these humans aren't after him for mundane reasons like a gambling or drug debt?"

Arik shrugged. "Thus far, attempts to question any have failed due to a lack of viable subjects."

"You haven't captured any?" A note of incredulity in her voice.

"More like none survived. The first one was shot by a sniper as we were trying to load him into the trunk. The last pair got hit by a semi truck during transport. Luckily, our driver walked away with barely a scratch. No matter where, they end up dying in our grasp. We appear to have a mole in our midst."

Her mouth rounded. A traitor. The very idea. "No."

"It's happened too many times now to be a coincidence."

"How have those attack parties been armed?"

"With bullets and tranquilizers. It's our belief they're working with a female bear, name of Lada."

"How can anyone be in cahoots with *them*?" She couldn't help the repugnance. Humans were the ultimate threat to their survival. To find a shifter betrayed that simple precept...

Arik shrugged. "That's what we need to find out. All this interest in Peter began over an old key. If you see or hear anything about it, anything at all, let me know at once."

This job was looking more and more interesting. "Anything else?"

"Be careful. These humans we've encountered aren't messing around."

"I'll make sure I'm locked and loaded."

"I know I can count on you, Nora. Be careful. The people we're dealing with have acted rashly in the past, and I worry they might escalate."

She almost tossed her bobbed mane in disdain. Humans against a lioness? She'd wager on herself each and every time.

Things moved fast after that conversation. Too fast for her to say anything to the biatches as she packed a suitcase, filled up some grocery bins with goods, and tossed in a potted plant for good measure.

She arrived at her temporary home with a carload of boxes, bins, and bags. Zachary was on hand to unload them. He played the part of boyfriend well. He was a nice guy. Steady. Solid. Handsome if you liked your men rugged like granite and surly to those he didn't like.

"Hey, short stuff," was his greeting.

They did a pretend hug, and she whispered, "I take it the subject is inside."

"Hasn't moved all day."

"What floor?"

"One above us." Zach opened her trunk and began loading up on bins, the fabric handles letting him tote a few in each hand.

She carried her plant and rolled a large suitcase.

Entering, she noticed the elevator and the staircase. Usually she took the stairs, but that would be a bitchy thing for a girlfriend to do to her loaded down "boyfriend." Not that Zach would complain, but it would seem odd.

In the elevator, she pried more information. "Guess I get day shift 'cause of my job."

"Yup. I left you the big bedroom since it will be quieter at night when I'm doing my thing." His thing being on the lookout for anything out of the ordinary. During quiet moments, he'd pore over the day's footage, looking to see if anything was missed.

Their apartment had a painted brown door with a peephole. Three doors on each side of the hall for a total of six apartments per floor.

Zach unlocked it, and they entered the basic space. First a hall with doors leading off of it, including the bedroom with attached bath. At the end of the hall, a living room with couch, low-slung table. A big chair and moveable desk set up with three screens took pride of place. Right off the living room was the kitchen with its breakfast bar and high-top dining set in chrome.

Nicer than a few places she'd had to do surveillance in. "Give me a second to drop this, and we'll go over the case," she said. The plant and suitcase went into the bedroom, the corner apartment unit having a window that overlooked the alley and the fire escape.

She emerged to find Zach in his spot, hands moving, headset on, all his screens showing different things.

"What's our target been doing?"

Zach pointed to the video screen. "Montgomery hasn't left that chair where he's been reading a book."

She squinted at the tome in her target's hands. "*Hitchhiker's Guide to the Galaxy*? What kind of nerdy shit is that?"

Zach shrugged. "The kind that means an easy job."

"Boring." While male lions might like napping all the time—the grumpy Zach being no exception—she still wanted to be in on the action.

"I take it you've read the file on Montgomery?" She slipped into calling him by his last name.

"Yeah. Have you?"

Not yet but she planned to. In these days of modernity, his entire dossier had been sent via encrypted file to her phone. She stalled rather than read, preferring to get her own impression first rather than go in with a preconceived notion.

Since it was the weekend, Montgomery didn't work or shower. He played video games. Texted a few times. Had some chips around three and then ordered dinner at five. It looked yummy enough that Nora got the same thing.

By the time she went to bed, he'd gone from reading to online casino gaming. When she woke, it was to get a report from Zach that the man had gamed until three.

During her turn, Montgomery slept until noon then got up and read some more. But then, rather than order in, he showered and dressed, obviously prepping to leave. Meaning she had to wake Zach. "Subject is on the move," she told him.

"Fuck. Okay. I'm up," the big man said, rubbing his face. "Where's he going?"

"Given he doesn't have a car and didn't call for a ride, I'm guessing not far." And then, because she was bored and not getting anywhere, she decided it was time to officially run into Montgomery.

She quickly changed and raced down the stairs, knowing she had to beat the elevator. When her target emerged onto the ground floor, Nora was ass up in the lobby doing some stretches.

What she didn't understand was the warmth that enveloped her the moment his scent hit her. Strong spicy soap and male musk.

Tasty.

Mine.

CHAPTER TWO

He was only human.

Peter stopped and stared at the nice ass. Firm and round, encased in a pair of those black leggings everyone was so fond of. Perfect height for tapping, if he was a perv.

He walked past it. He knew better than to get involved with someone living in the same building. He'd made that mistake years ago. An ex-girlfriend, drunk out of her mind, pounding on the door at three a.m. while the new girlfriend was blowing him meant he didn't get to finish.

Nice Ass Lady caught up to him just as he opened the entrance door. A sense of politeness ingrained in him even after more than three decades on this Earth meant he held it and gestured. "After you."

"Thanks." She gave him a small smile and a dismissive glance as she shoved earbuds into her ears. Then off she went, jogging up the street, those tight glutes hypnotic.

He followed at a slower rate, hands in pockets, alert to everything around him. Paranoid as fuck despite his sister's boyfriend assuring him he had nothing to worry about.

As if Lawrence knew for sure. He might have found Peter in that hospital and gotten him off the drugs they were pumping him with, but once they cleared his system, the memories of why they'd drugged him returned. He couldn't even look at a box of the original and only Frosted Flakes without getting a shiver.

There was a time the mere recollection of orange and black stripes would send him into a screaming fit, the kind that brought men in white coats to lock him away. In that padded room he was safe. The tiger surely couldn't get at him in there.

Eventually the panic stopped. He started to sleep. Remembered his name. Then he was found. Rescued at last, and while aware he'd suffered trauma, he told his sister, the doctors, everyone, that he didn't remember a thing.

He told Charlie, his sister, he was fine. She nagged him to go see a doctor to discuss possible post-traumatic stress. One screaming nightmare and she thought he had a problem. Was it any wonder after Charlie's honeymoon cruise—which he got dragged along on—he found himself an apartment far from his sister?

He loved her, but he couldn't stand the hovering. And then there was his lying. He felt guilty about that most of all. She'd uprooted her life and gone to Russia looking for him. Had put herself in danger. That more than anything made him wish he could rewind the clock.

But spilled milk and all that. There was nothing to do now about it. He'd survived. Charlie met the man of her dreams as a result of his actions, so silver lining. His sister was going to have a happy life.

As for him... He had to lie low. At least for a little while until he was sure his troubles were all over. So far, so good. He'd not seen a single tiger since arriving in the United States.

His neighbor pivoted at the corner and jogged back, barely acknowledging him as she ran past.

He briefly turned to watch her go.

The view was nice.

She passed him again. Apparently, she preferred to stick close to home when she ran. He saw her sweep past yet again as he entered the tavern for dinner. Just watching her exercise made him hungry.

As taverns went, it fit the standard bill; dark, dingy,

the booths high-backed and private where they sat bolted along the wall. The meals were actually more decent than the décor suggested. He shouldn't be picky given what he'd eaten recently. The institution where he'd spent a few weeks catching invisible butterflies was particularly fond of runny, flavorless gruel. As he learned, though, a stomach wasn't picky when it came to survival.

Only after he'd placed his order did he pull his phone from his pocket, VPN enabled to hide his activities. Most of it was innocuous shopping. Extra gaming remote, more coffee for his machine, random stuff that amounted to lots of tiny packages from multiple places, including two mailboxes he'd rented a while ago. Via a secured bitcoin account, he paid to have the mail forwarded. It and his purchases should arrive around the same time, muddling the two things he really wanted to get his hands on, despite those who might be watching.

Given his new brother-in-law helped him get the apartment, he had to wonder if his sister knew about the cameras inside. He'd spotted them the first day. Nicely hidden. Comprised of newer, camouflaging models. But they made the mistake of wireless transmission.

Signals could always be spied on, or hijacked.

Knowing someone was watching, Peter spent some time being very mundane. So far, he'd created hours of gaming, reading, and other boring stuff. Never knew when he might need to make a virtual copy of himself for watchers.

As to who was spying on him? Perhaps it was Lawrence, who had connections but wouldn't talk about them. Had his sister married into the mob?

Kind of cool if she had, so long as he didn't get on their bad side.

His gaze flickered to the tavern's main door as a huge guy walked in. Close-cropped hair and trimmed goatee, built like a linebacker. Peter stared a moment, trying to place why he seemed familiar. Hadn't he seen him from his living room window a few days ago, unloading boxes with the woman he'd seen jogging?

One of his new neighbors. He wondered if they got the same deal as him. Fully furnished apartment for less than he would have expected because his BIL knew the landlord.

Peter figured he was paying at least five hundred dollars under market, but he wasn't complaining about that or the job Lawrence found him working in a bookstore. Mind-numbing work that gave him a cover to hide his other activities and bide his time.

A few hours later, when he paid, he noticed the

neighbor had already left. Obviously not spying on him. Just like he doubted the pair of barflies—who'd arrived around the same time he did and were nursing their umpteenth beers—gave a fuck.

Paranoia was a step in the direction of the padded white room and the little pills that made him drool. Just like giving in to the urge to flinch every time he thought he saw the flick of a tail was giving in to the nightmares that plagued him.

He would be brave. There were no tigers in the city. No one left to hurt him.

He hoped.

Upon leaving the bar, he hit the sidewalk with a long stride and lost the few other pedestrians within the first block. He trudged along, hands in his pockets, head down. Both sides of the road were empty, and yet he felt watched. The skin between his shoulders prickled.

His hands flexed at the scuff of a shoe on pavement. He had nothing to defend himself with. A gun would have done the trick, but laws had tightened in recent years for this state. There was a waiting period now to own a legal weapon. He'd applied already, but these things took time. If he wanted something sooner, he'd have to make contact with the underworld where cash was king and the selection not always USA approved.

Not that he needed anything big or hardcore. Simply a revolver he could slip under his jacket. With a caliber big enough to take down an elephant. Enough to make him feel safe.

He passed by a closed electronics shop. The big window had televisions flashing, playing some kind of show with a bleach blond, mullet-wearing guy in a Hawaiian shirt hugging a tiger. Terrifying. He couldn't help but shudder as he walked faster.

He could have sworn he heard steps shadowing him. When he stopped, so did the echo.

Probably his imagination, yet he quickened his stride.

A car parked along the sidewalk, dark and engine off, suddenly popped its trunk. It might as well have been a gunshot.

Heart suddenly pounding, Peter darted into an alley, where a thick miasma of garbage hit him. Gag worthy but he soldiered through. Having memorized the routes to his apartment ahead of time, he knew this dark corridor led to a bright thoroughfare and a donut shop popular with the boys in blue.

Thump. Thump. Familiar meaty sounds of violence that only made him run faster.

He hit the street at the far end, saw the red and blue lights on a cruiser, and heaved a sigh of relief before looking over his shoulder to see…no one there.

Another false alarm. Would he forever live his life looking over his shoulder?

He hoped not. Reaching his apartment, he shut his door and deadbolted it. He wanted to check the windows even though they had no means of being reached. Resisted the urge to drop to his knees and look under the couch.

Couldn't let those watching see how close he teetered on the edge.

It wasn't late enough for bed, so he texted his sister.

Rather than reply, she called. "Peter, peter, pumpkin eater," she sang, sounding so happy.

"How's my favorite sister doing?"

"I'm your only sister."

"Are you implying you need competition to be the best sister there is?"

She laughed. "Still an idiot."

"Love you too," he teased. "Any particular reason why you're calling?"

"Actually, yes. It's about that stupid key we found in your apartment. Lawrence's aunts were bugging me about it again."

"Did you tell them I don't remember anything?" It was the line he kept to over and over.

"I have, over and over, but they seem to think if maybe they could talk to you in person, you might remember something."

Like fuck. He'd met enough of Lawrence's family and friends to know there was something a little off about the group. Not appearance wise. He'd never seen a fitter, more attractive bunch. But something in the way they moved and eyed the world and people around them freaked him the fuck out.

"I wish I could help. I didn't even know there was a key hidden in my apartment. It must have been left there by the previous occupant." He lied his ass off and felt a twinge at deceiving his sister. However, in his defense, if he told her what he knew, she'd tell her husband, and then shit would get tense.

"If you say so," was her doubtful reply.

"Gotta go. Work in the morning." More like he hated lying to Charlie. He hung up. Then, because of those fucking cameras, had to pretend he wasn't agitated.

Problem being, he *was* fucking agitated. Only one thing to do.

He went looking for kittens.

Which might sound odd until tried. Something about the cute little furballs was relaxing and soothed him. Maybe one day he'd adopt one and not have to leave his house for calming. Today was not that day.

He found a lapful of furballs in the alley not far from the dry cleaners. He stroked the little rumbling bodies and couldn't help thinking of the key found in his apartment in Russia. Everyone wanted to get their hands on it.

Let them. By the time they figured out the truth, he'd hopefully already have the treasure in hand.

CHAPTER THREE

Nora didn't find out about the attempted Montgomery kidnapping until the next morning. Night-shift Zach, who'd taken over surveillance so she could sleep, didn't think to wake her.

He told her about it over the protein shake he'd made her for breakfast. Something gross and full of stuff that belonged in a rabbit cage, making them fat for eating. He ended up wearing some green goo as she spat it out and exclaimed, "What the hell? Why didn't you wake me?"

"Didn't see the point since I thwarted their attempt." Zach dabbed at the slime rolling down his shirt.

It didn't appear to be chewing through fabric. Yet. Her stomach, though…it rebelled against all that healthy stuff in one shot.

"Are you sure they were after him?" she asked.

"Sure seemed like it. The trunk on that car opened just seconds before Montgomery would have passed it. There were two guys in the car, one in the front, one in the back. The guy in the rear seat is the one who jumped out the second our boy went into the alley."

"The same alley you were hiding in?"

He nodded. "Good thing I was already watching from the fire escape."

"Where did you stash the perps? I want to talk to them."

"I don't have them." His lips turned down. "I knocked out the backseat guy and would have taken front seat out, too, if a patrol car didn't turn onto the street."

Since getting arrested was a big no-no, Zach had darted back into the alley and watched as the driver hauled his friend off.

She inadvertently took a swig of the toxic green stuff and managed to swallow rather than gag. She had an ex-boyfriend who would have been impressed. "Did you get the license plate?"

"Yeah. And I already ran it. It's a fake."

"What about Montgomery? Is he aware of what happened? Did he see you?"

"No and no. He made it back to his apartment safe." He pointed to the screen.

Montgomery was just getting out of bed, wearing nothing but black briefs. Much sexier than those baggy shorts some guys wore as underwear.

If Montgomery followed his routine, he'd be in the bathroom for about forty-five minutes and would emerge showered and wrapped in a towel from his waist down. For a human, he had a decent body. Lean. Too lean, actually, and more muscled than a sedentary guy like him had any business owning.

Almost as intriguing as the vee leading below the towel's edge were the scars. White stripes all over his body. Old scars healed, but caused by what? They indicated he'd not spent the last six months in a luxury situation, but no one knew where he'd been.

Nora had pored over his file. It painted an interesting picture.

Peter Montgomery had a rap sheet. Theft being highest on his list. Nothing violent or truly depraved. He did like antiques, though. Not as a collector but as a person who acquired and then resold them for what the art world claimed they were worth. He'd had two lawsuits filed against him in the past for not disclosing the fact he knew something was valuable and giving the owners peanuts for it. Not exactly a crime if morally unethical, as one judge claimed before tossing the case.

In the case of the jail time he'd done, it was a heist

gone wrong with him left as the fall guy. He got out and was later suspected of a few crimes, nothing concrete. Then about six months ago, he'd traveled to Russia on business. What business was never gleaned. He'd gone missing long enough that his sister went over to look for him. She didn't find Montgomery, but she did get embroiled in a mystery that involved a key recovered from his apartment in Russia.

A key he supposedly didn't remember. A disappearance that left him with amnesia. And scars…

Didn't need to be curious to realize there was something hinky about the whole thing.

"What are you hiding?" she muttered before getting ready to go to work.

She got into place just in time and was checking the mailbox when he emerged from the elevator onto the ground floor. She leaned into the metal array of locked boxes, peering as she reached for nothing. He left without a word of greeting, and thirty seconds later, so did she. In bright daylight with people around, an attack was less likely. Especially since Zach had thwarted one just the night before. Whoever was targeting Montgomery would need to regroup.

Her subject didn't have to go far before he entered a bookstore that matched his nerdy pastimes since they'd started spying, but not his portfolio of crimes. Which was the real man? The guy who'd pulled off some clever heists or the one who probably owned a set of dice and a wizard's robe?

With him at work, it was time for her to start her new job. She entered the butcher shop that dealt in deli meats along with the fresher stuff. It resided across from the bookstore. Owned by some panther shifters under Pride protection, they'd agreed to let her pretend to work for them. It provided opportunities to go outside to wash the big display window. An hour later, she swept the sidewalk, watching who stayed parked too long. Who loitered. Every time someone entered his store, an alarm pinged her, and she also got notice if the door on the alley opened. Melly had installed special security to help Nora keep track of those coming and going. Brisker traffic than she would have expected for such a small shop. Nora wasn't big on the whole reading thing, but she did like video gaming. First-person shooter and fighting scenarios being her faves.

Which happened to be what her target played.

Not that she cared about his likes. He was a job.

When he left the shop around noon, she started untying her apron, only to realize he was crossing the road. Shit, he was coming into the shop.

Why? Had he pegged her? How should she handle it?

Probably by pretending she actually worked here.

She busied herself behind the counter, straightening the cheese slices, because you know, a good sandwich needed them tidy?

He'd think she was an idiot for sure. Next she'd be aligning the slices of meat.

She tucked her hands behind her back. "Hello and welcome. Can I help you?" The standard greeting she'd heard many a time when entering a place of business.

"Hey. Don't I know you?"

Given they'd seen each other a few times around the building, lying was out of the question. "Maybe. You live around here?"

"That's it." He lifted his finger in an aha moment. "You're the new neighbor."

"Am I?" She played it nonchalant.

"You like to jog, and your boyfriend is into computers."

So he'd noticed. "Do you stalk all your neighbors, or am I just special?" she crooned, leaning forward on the counter.

The query threw him off balance, but not for long. "You exercise and make food. Of course, I noticed."

She laughed. "You assume I can cook."

"You don't?"

"Not much. But I do make a mean toast."

"You're scaring me about the lunch special."

"We have a special?" she blurted out. She'd studied it, and yet she couldn't remember what it was. His presence oddly frazzled.

He pointed, and she turned her head to see a chalkboard. Written on it in big letters was the name of the special and what it contained: basic sandwich, drink, and a side.

"Oh, you mean that special." Way to cover. She kept her hands laced behind her back. "What will it be?"

"I'm not sure. What do you recommend?"

He wanted a suggestion? Shit. Did they have a menu? She glanced behind her. Saw nothing.

He cleared his throat. "I take it you're new."

"How can you tell?" was her sarcastic reply.

"Then let me help you out. I tell you what goes on the sandwich, you make it."

"You, a man, want me, a woman, to make you a sandwich? I see the patriarchy is alive and well."

He choked and covered it with a hand. "I just assumed that was part of your job description given you're behind the counter and health laws forbid a customer from serving themselves."

"I guess in this case, it's okay," she said begrudging, because she really didn't want this expectation of her making food to persist. She liked her stuff readymade.

"Thank you? I think," was his bemused reply. He

took a moment to eye the deli meat selection, hands shoved into his pockets, hair askew as if he'd been in a strong wind. Maybe the flapping of book pages?

"I'll have a pastrami on rye, easy on the mustard, with cheddar, please. And a bag of chips." He pointed.

Seemed easy enough. As she went to grab the bun, she remembered to wash her hands, mostly because there was a sign right above the bread screaming, Wash First. Right over the little sink was a box of gloves. Ick. She wasn't rectally probing a sandwich, just making it.

The knife-wielding part she had fun with, tossing the bun in the air and trying to slice, only the dull blade failed. The bun fell, hit the edge of her counter, and hit the floor. She eyed the bun and then Montgomery. "Guess I should get another one?"

He sounded quite choked as he said, "Yes, please."

She kept a firm grip on the bun this time and sawed it jaggedly into two. Made a mental note to bring a sharper knife.

"That's not rye."

"Get over it." She eyed the whole-wheat interior. Now what? She glanced at the array of bottles, hand hovering until he said, "I like it with mustard in a zigzag first."

She grabbed the yellow bottle, hoped she guessed right, and to be contrary, did a big circle on each bun. Then for good measure, added an N with a flourish.

"What does the N stand for?" he asked.

"Nora."

"Good to know. Next, let's add some veggies."

She wrinkled her nose. "You really want to ruin it that way?"

"What do you suggest?"

"Cheese. Then meat. Don't take away from the meat!" She tossed on some orange cheese slices, layering it three deep. Who cut them too thin?

He talked as he watched her layering on the pastrami—which had a label!—like she'd enjoy eating. Thick to reduce the ratio of bread.

"So you like to jog."

"Guilty," she said, adding even more meat since the bread was the poufy kind. Eyed a pickle and wondered if she dared add it. It counted as a vegetable, which he might like. As if she cared. Still... She threw a line of pickles into it then lifted it to hand over.

"Are you going to wrap it first?"

"You're difficult," she grumbled as he added yet another step to the process. Who knew food took so long? No wonder she preferred having it made for her.

As she placed the sandwich in the paper, she wondered where they kept the larger pieces, since it wasn't big enough to wrap around.

"Where did you move from?" Wasn't he just a Chatty Cathy today?

"East End." Technically true, the false part being she'd not really moved. All of her stuff remained in her condo, like her bed, which she really missed.

"And you're on the floor below me with your boyfriend."

It might have been the boredom that made her purr, "Why are you asking? Interested?" She leaned forward and batted her lashes. It would have worked better with a lower-cut shirt, and maybe not having the stench of meat stuck to her as she handed him his sandwich, mummied in several pieces of paper.

"Interested?" He appeared startled. "Fuck no."

"That's a little harsh." She couldn't help a moue of discontent.

"Not because of you. A man would have to be stupid to get in the way of your refrigerator-sized partner."

Her lips twitched. He had a valid point. "Lucky for you Zach isn't the jealous type." All the jobs they'd done together and not once had there been the slightest spark.

"You'd cheat on your boyfriend?" He, the career criminal, sounded shocked.

She rolled her shoulders. "We have an understanding."

He snorted. "Yeah. I'd never be into that."

"What *are* you into?" She gave it a husky note.

"I'm into getting the rest of my lunch. I'll have those barbecue chips and a bottle of iced tea."

"Everyone knows salt and vinegar is the best," she said as she grabbed the items and handed them over.

"I'll remember that for next time. See you later, Nora." He tossed a ten on the counter and walked out.

She almost went after him.

CHAPTER FOUR

That afternoon Nora wondered what he meant by later. Today? Tomorrow? Maybe he just said it because it was the thing to say. Not because he meant it.

She'd screwed up royally. How could she get close to him if he wanted nothing to do with her?

His replacement arrived at five o'clock. Rather than head home, Montgomery again crossed the road for the butcher shop!

"Back so soon?" she said lightly as he entered.

"What can I say, the service is impeccable."

She almost snorted. "You want another sandwich?" Which she'd learned wasn't supposed to have a proper three inches of meat. The owner, Pamela, had almost fainted when she saw the size of the sandwiches Nora kept making.

"That sandwich was epic. But I'm thinking something different for tonight. I'm in the mood for some steak." He pointed to a bacon-wrapped filet mignon. "Two of those, and two of the double-stuffed baked potatoes."

Enough to make a snack for her, but for a human? Two portions could mean, "Hot date tonight?" she asked.

"Nope. Just really hungry."

"Maybe you should get a sandwich, too, just in case."

"That one you made me for lunch was pretty big. But good. Maybe another for a snack."

Pamela emerged from the back with a snarl. "You're done. I got this. You can go."

"Sweet. See ya," she said to Peter, pulling off her apron.

As she went to leave, the bell over the door jingled and a woman walked in. She beamed the moment she saw Montgomery.

"Peter!"

"Hey, Heather. How's it going?"

Heather batted her lashes as if trying to take off for flight. "Going good. So nice to see you again."

And the jerk, who'd soundly rejected Nora because she had a fake boyfriend, gave Heather a dimpled smile. "And you. We really should get together for that drink."

Heather barely waited for him to finish. "How about Friday after work? Dinner first?" The lashes fluttered so hard Nora was sure she saw liftoff.

She couldn't delay any more without making it obvious she was staring. Leaving her apron behind but grabbing her purse, she headed for the door. Montgomery sprang forward to hold it open for her.

"Thanks," she muttered, brushing past. Awareness filled her, and inside there was a rumble.

Tasty.

Her inner feline must mean the steak she could smell. Perhaps she should have ordered some food too. But that would mean going back in and watching Montgomery flirting with that vapid brunette.

Everyone knew blondes were better. Real ones. She tossed her head.

She also popped into the Chinese place next door, placed an order, and stood near the window to keep watch while waiting for it. Montgomery exited, bag in hand, still talking to Heather. Probably concreting their date plans.

Grrr.

"It's ready." Two brown bags were shoved at her. She'd made sure to get some for Zach. One bag in each hand, she exited the store, purposefully not looking toward Montgomery, who still chatted with Heather.

What could they have to talk about?

Her agitated walk soon had company, as Montgomery suddenly appeared by her side.

"Chinese? You're making me rethink my steak decision."

"What's your *girlfriend* having?" She could have slapped herself for the tone she injected in that word.

"Heather? Definitely not girlfriend material."

"I thought you were making a date for Friday." Too late she realized it showed she'd been listening.

"A man has needs."

"You'd use her for sex?"

"We'd use each other. Not a big deal."

"If sex isn't a big deal, then why disparage me when I said Zach and I had an open arrangement?"

"Because casual sex is one thing. If there's another person involved, it gets messy."

"Fair enough." She'd seen jealousy. Never really suffered it much, although she did have a competitive streak.

"So what does your boyfriend do with all those computers?"

"He's a programmer."

"And gets to work from home, which is nice.

Pajamas all day and no one stealing your food from the fridge."

"I thought you worked alone." Again, her tongue slipped away, but he didn't seem to notice that she'd been paying attention.

"How did you find the job at the butcher shop?"

"Family connections," she explained with a shrug.

"Yeah, same for me too. My sister's hubby helped me with that and the apartment."

"Got to say a bookstore wouldn't have been my first choice." Her nose wrinkled.

"Says the woman slinging meat."

"I like meat. The way it feels in my mouth. The taste. The chewing and succulence." She cast him a glance from the corner of her eye. Caught him looking right back with a half-grin.

"I'm more a sweets kind of guy. Nothing better than something delicious to lick, maybe suckle and savor."

Would he fight if she dragged him into the alley to ask for a demonstration?

No playing with her target. What if she broke him?

"Is being a bookseller your dream job?" she found herself asking to veer the conversation.

"No, that would be lying on a beach."

"Not sure how it would pay the bills."

"Money is the only thing holding me back," he said, holding open the door to their building.

"You the kind who buys lottery tickets hoping to strike it rich?"

"Forget hope. I will one day be wealthy. Evening, Nora." He paused by the mailbox.

Since she'd checked that morning, she thought it might look odd if she did it again. Instead, she went for the stairs but hung just inside the door, listening, just in case someone followed Montgomery in.

She heard the elevator ding as the doors opened. Then hum as it moved. A quick peek showed the entrance empty.

Arriving in her apartment, she dumped the Chinese food and got a plate out to pile some on it. As she wandered to the screens with it heaped high, she realized her subject hadn't gone home. The monitors showed no movement, not inside his place or the hall. And the elevator had no one on board.

"Fuck!" she exclaimed. Montgomery had given her the slip.

She quickly headed back out, racing down those steps, having to slow down rather than burst out onto the street. She glanced both ways and didn't see any sign of him.

Arik would have her head if she'd lost Montgomery. Hell, she wasn't too impressed with herself right now.

She caught his scent, faint but present, and followed it in the opposite direction from which they'd just arrived. It went to the liquor store, and before she could pretend to walk past it, he exited, appeared startled, and said, "Hey."

She eyed the brown bag with meat in his hand and the plastic one with the liquor store's log on it. He'd gone to buy some booze. She quickly covered her gaffe. "Great minds, I see." She offered a weak smile. "What's your poison?"

"Red wine for the steaks. You?"

"I'm thinking it's a good night for margaritas."

"Enjoy." He slipped sideways, and she could really make this worse by following him, or she could get in and out as fast as possible. It still took a few minutes, and by the time she emerged, Peter was gone again. But this time, when she got back to the apartment, she saw him on the screen, broiling his steaks and potatoes in the oven, pouring himself a glass of red wine. Making her drool despite the Chinese feast spread out around her.

As he sat down to eat, she could have sworn he glanced at the camera in the corner by the air vent. He held his glass in the air a little longer than necessary, as if saluting. He definitely winked.

Did he know someone watched? Impossible.

But the next day she really had to wonder because when she didn't see Montgomery leaving the store when his shift finished, she wandered over to the bookstore, only to realize he'd slipped her again.

He was unaccounted for over two hours. He returned with a bag of takeout, and she could have sworn he wore a smirk as he leaned in his chair, eyeing the camera.

Oh yeah, he knew.

Game on.

CHAPTER FIVE

He was in Irina's house, facing off against the tiger.

Again.

He knew it was a dream, more like a flashback, one that liked to repeat itself over and over.

Then he was in the car. The tiger leaped and somehow missed his hood. He swerved to avoid it and took off. He kept checking his rearview mirror, expecting at any second to see an orange and black cat running after him.

Impossible. A tiger couldn't match the speed of a car. Still, he didn't ease up on the gas until he reached the bright lights of the city. It didn't take much time to make the trip this time of night, although street parking proved to be a challenge. Eventually, he entered his apartment without seeing a single tiger.

He pulled out the key. The metal was cold enough he couldn't hold it for long. He dropped it with a clang onto the table and went to bed.

The next day, he woke late morning. He peered out the window and saw a guy standing across from it, cigarette dangling from his lips, appearing to stare right at his window. Not that he'd see anything. The glare of light would prevent him from seeing in. Peter kept an eye out and could have sworn the same guy in different spots smoked and watched. First in a ball cap, then a hoodie, then nothing but his bald head.

He told himself he was being paranoid. No one was spying on him.

He fired off a message to the people who wanted to buy the key. Let them have it. He couldn't stand touching it for long. Funny how the fake key he'd had made, so similar in appearance, didn't give him the same feeling. It didn't make him shiver.

The buyers replied with instructions, and that was when they started pulling some shit. Rather than paying half now, half on the trade, they wanted to do the whole amount only once he handed over the key. Smelled like a double cross to him. He messaged them back and said half now, or no key.

The money arrived not long after, but the trust was gone. He wrapped the key in used panties, put it into an envelope, and mailed it to himself in the States. The return address was for a prostitute who also had a side hustle in worn garments.

The fake was stashed in a hidey-hole. The day after he handed it over, he had a flight booked to take him home. He'd be on a plane by tomorrow night.

That night he woke to heavy breathing. Huff. Huff. Huff.

It reminded him of an animal. Impossible. Unless a rat got inside his apartment.

Huff. Huff. Huff.

He was being dumb. No one could be inside. He'd locked his door and windows. It was probably something stupid like in that segment on America's Funniest Home Videos where the mind conjured up all kinds of weird things at sounds that turned out to be innocuous.

Just in case, though, he reached for the gun he kept under his pillow, only to have something slam into him. Teeth grazed his throat, paws with claws pressed into his shoulders.

In his dream, he relived over and over the unmanly whimper that emerged from him. Relived the terror.

The tiger had found him.

It would have been easier if it had mauled him to death then and there.

The dream always fast-forwarded at that point until he was inside the cage. Too short to stand. A bucket sat in the corner. And most worrisome of all, the old lady stood in front of it, wrapped in a robe, hair crazy, eyes even crazier.

But it was the things she did to him, the things she made him think he saw...

Peter woke twisted in his sheets. Sweating. Heart pounding. Fear clenching him tight. It took him a moment to calm himself from the nightmare.

Nothing new. Apparently quite normal given he'd gone through something traumatic. Blah. Blah. He just wanted to stop being afraid all the fucking time.

Then again, his paranoia might save his life. He thought he was going nuts again when he convinced himself the new neighbors were spying on him. To prove himself wrong, he ran a small test. Decided to run to the liquor store, leaving Nora behind.

As he browsed for a bottle, he'd wondered if she'd be the one following him or her beefy partner. Or he was wrong and she wasn't spying on him, just a flirty woman—with baggage.

However, his sixth sense proved right. He walked out of the store and startled his cute neighbor. No denying she was keeping an eye on him. The question being, was Nora following him because of his sister, or was it the people he'd screwed out of the key?

After all, he'd received partial payment, but they never got what they paid for. They never would. He'd not suffered to fail now.

Since he couldn't trust anyone, possibly not even his sister, there was only one thing to do. Move on.

First, he rolled out of bed and hit the bathroom, the one place without a camera. Did they know what he could do with his phone in there?

The footage he'd hijacked previously now came into play. The video stream was pushed into the live feed so that whoever watched wouldn't see what he was actually doing. Packing to leave.

The heavy metal key, still just as shivery cold, went into an inner pocket of his knapsack, one with a zipper so it wouldn't accidentally fall out, along with a flint and some chalk. In the larger section went his clothes, extra footwear, and protein bars. He would have taken the old book of fairytales with him; however, at its age and size, the pictures he'd stored in a cloud online would be more practical. The book itself he kept tucked inside the linen cabinet, between the folds of a towel. It would be found if someone tore his place apart, but he couldn't bring himself to destroy it. The thing was priceless. The cover, the pages, every illustration and text done by hand. No one even suspected he had the original.

Just like no one knew he had the real key. He'd kept them busy chasing the fake that someone finally located inside his apartment. Meanwhile, the original waited for him in a postal box back home.

With all his things packed, including his passport with his new fake name, Peter swung the knapsack on his back and then climbed out of his window onto the fire escape. He didn't dare use his front door. Time for a stealthy escape since he didn't want his shadow tailing him.

Not where he was going.

He thought he'd made a clean getaway until the morning after his arrival in Switzerland when he woke to a weight on his chest and a purring voice that said, "Where do you think you're going, Peter?"

CHAPTER SIX

Rather than reply to her query, Peter asked one of his own. "What the fuck are you doing following me, *Nora*?"

She'd yet to ease the pressure on him. It should be noted, she enjoyed the position a little more than she should. "Why did you run, Peter?

"Maybe because I don't like being spied on."

"When did you figure out I was watching you?"

"The sandwich was when I got suspicious."

"Why is everyone freaking out about that damned sandwich?" Pamela had lectured her a few more times about economics and profits and other boring stuff that amounted to make the sandwiches puny or else.

"You and that job weren't well suited."

"Neither were you and yours," she sassed right back.

"You're right, it wasn't." He grinned, a little too cute and boyish.

She wouldn't let him fool her again. She kept her guard up. "Most people don't assume they're being watched."

"Unless you're a man in my position. Not to mention your cameras were less than discreet."

She grimaced. "The best they could manage on short notice."

"They?"

"You don't really expect me to answer that, do you?"

"No. But you did just confirm you were hired. Hopefully with a discount given you were less than subtle."

The dig might have stung more if it were false. Problem was he'd intrigued her from afar and she'd wanted to get close. And now that she pinned him, she wanted to get even closer. "Subtlety is not a requirement for my job." Not entirely true. After Arik freaked out on her, assuming she'd messed up, he'd told her to do whatever it took to find Peter and then stick to him like glue. As for Zach, he took apart the apartment Peter left behind.

"A job for who? Who do you work for?"

"Still not telling," she sang, wondering when he'd attempt to get out from under her.

"Is it my sister? Her husband?" he insisted.

"Does it matter? It's obvious there's a few groups of people interested in you."

"And yet I am a boring guy."

"Hardly. Although you did a good job trying to make us think you were. How many times did you switch out the feed so you could do your thing?"

His lips quirked. "Wouldn't you like to know."

"It was clever," she admitted. "And might be handy to know in the future."

"A magician never reveals his secrets."

"You're hardly magical," she said with a snort.

"And yet I eluded you and your partner numerous times. Tell me, where is the big guy? Hiding outside in the hall? Keeping the getaway car warm? Drilling a hole in the wall from the room next to this one?"

"It's just me and you, Montgomery."

"Montgomery? And here I thought we'd reached first name status," was his sarcastic reply.

"Would you prefer I call you Peter? After all, you and I are about to become close friends."

"No, we're not."

Funny because his racing heart and hard-on said otherwise. She straddled him, ignoring the cheap thrill the pressure put on her parts. "Where are you going?"

"No idea. I got itchy feet and decided I wanted to wander."

"Could that wandering have to do with a certain book and key?"

He stiffened, and not just his dick this time. "I don't know what you're talking about."

"Don't you?"

"If I could read women's minds, I'd be rich." he tried to joke. It fell flat.

"Are you really going to make this hard?" And yes, she might have pressed down on him. Saw his eyes dilate, his lips part. He definitely twitched.

He didn't give in. "Why are you watching me?"

"I'm the one asking questions here."

"Then ask ones that I can actually reply to. I know nothing about a book and key."

"I really wish you'd skip the lying part," she said with a sigh. She held up the ugly, heavy key that gave her an uncomfortable shiver. She'd scrounged it out of his pack while he slept.

His eyes narrowed in anger. "Give that back. It's mine.

"Is it? Or did you steal it?" She kept it out of reach when he would have grabbed it.

"I went through a lot to get that fucking key."

"No kidding, given it was supposed to have been washed away when Lada dropped it into the river." The realization hit her suddenly. "That wasn't the real key."

"And if it wasn't?"

"Holy shit. People died because of that fake. You put your sister in danger because of it."

He grimaced. "It wasn't meant to fall into her hands. I intended for it to act as a decoy to throw people off my trail."

"It worked." All too well, given the people who'd died trying to get their paws on it. "And just so you know, Zach has the book." A grimoire-style tome containing an old fairytale and an image of the highly-in-demand key.

"Good for him. I assume he knows how to read medieval Russian?"

"Not yet, but he'll find someone who can. Or you could make this easy and tell us what the book says."

"Fuck you. I am not telling you shit," he snarled. Still very human with the courage of a lion. Which explained the marks on his body. And the nightmares.

"Those six months you were missing… Someone was trying to get you to spill your guts."

"What gave it away?"

"I've seen your scars."

His expression turned blank. "Those weren't because of the key."

"Even if they weren't, you need to listen to me when I say you're in deep trouble. You're messing with some dangerous people, Peter."

His sarcasm was thick as he replied, "Ya think?"

"I can help."

"Help?" He snorted. "What I need is for you and the giant to stay away from me so I can blend in."

"No can do. We've already thwarted one kidnapping attempt. You need me to stick close by."

He blinked at her. "Repeat that. Slowly. With context."

"The other night, someone wanted to shove you into a trunk, but Zach saved you."

"Says you."

"Yeah says me, and it wasn't the first attempt. Count yourself lucky your sister married into the right family. We know how to protect our own."

"She did marry into the mob. I fucking knew it," he exclaimed.

Whereas Nora laughed. "Not quite, but close."

"So what exactly is your job?"

"In your case? Think of me as your bodyguard and partner."

"And thief." He indicated the key she still held.

It hadn't yet warmed in her grip. Weird metal.

"You are under the misconception I need money." She leaned close so her hot breath fanned his mouth. "I don't."

"Says the girl working in a butcher shop and taking shitty undercover work."

"Says the girl who is independently wealthy and seeks to stave off boredom."

"I don't believe you."

"Don't care." She shrugged. "It is true though. And can you blame me? It was undercover PI stuff or putting on a suit and going to an office every day."

"Fuck the suits."

"Exactly."

"And fuck you. I don't need a partner." He shoved at her, and she rolled off of him, lying on his bed as he stood, mostly dressed, his T-shirt rumpled like his hair, his pants unbuttoned. Ready to flee at a moment's notice.

She held up his key. "You either work with me, or I find someone else to help me figure it out."

"There is no one else," he growled.

"You're not the only one who knows of the story surrounding this key. As we speak, efforts are being made to translate the book we found in your apartment." The quick and dirty summary gleaned by images placed it as a fairytale along the lines of Frog Prince, except in this case, the hero, who was a monster, went on a quest to find magic to make him human. Sounded more like a nightmare to her.

"Good luck with finding out anything." He smirked.

"I don't need luck since Melly got me access to your cloud."

That got his attention. "Bullshit. It's heavily encrypted."

"Yeah, did I mention I'm friends with a hacker?" Her turn to smile and bluff because while Melly knew he had a secret online storage space, she was still working on getting in.

"You're lying."

"Am I?" She rolled off the bed and stalked toward him. "I mean it when I say work with me or be left out of the equation."

She could see the inner battle taking place reflected on his face before resignation softened it. "Fine. You win. But only if you promise I get to keep whatever we find."

"Sure." Another lie, because if it was dangerous to her kind, Peter wouldn't live to tell about it. "What are we looking for?"

"The next clue."

"For what?"

He just lifted a brow.

"It's in this city?"

"Why do you think I flew here first? We need to visit a church."

"Feeling a need to commune with God?"

"More like have a chat with the dead. How do you feel about visiting a crypt?"

"I've always wanted to star in a horror movie," she quipped. "Lead the way, Montgomery."

It was actually thirty minutes before they left the hotel, with him insisting on a shower first. Then they stopped at a street vendor to grab some fresh pastries, plus a coffee for him and a hot cocoa for her.

Her grumpy companion let her pay for everything, including the entrance fee to the old church. The interior was a masterpiece of intricately patterned plaster, vaulted ceilings, and stained glass.

Humans and their religion. The only thing Nora believed in was the might of her Pride and the blessing of the moon.

Even at this early hour, there was a group of people waiting to enter the catacombs. Peter and Nora joined them, close but not touching, him doing his best to ignore her, and yet she couldn't seem to do the same.

The man drew her, yet she couldn't have pinpointed why exactly. His looks? He had a ruggedness she really liked. A sense of humor she totally got. A pull that gave her an urge to rub up against him and mark him with her scent. As if her inner feline wanted to own him. Except a human wasn't a pet like that mink she'd adopted when she was young. Although she'd bet he'd be fun to play with. If she was gentle. Non-shifters were fragile that way.

The tour group descended an old set of stone steps, a groove worn into them by time and the tread of many feet. It forced them to cluster close together. She gritted her teeth against so many people in her space. Strangers that she wanted to bat aside.

She did turn her head and hiss as someone's hand ended up on her ass. Her glare had the fellow behind her pretending innocence. If he grabbed her again, she'd break his hand.

Peter noticed and, with a frown, stepped closer. Funny how she didn't mind when he brushed up against her. Hell, she wanted to get closer to him.

The tour group funneled through the narrow catacombs as the guide droned on, spitting out dates and names that had no meaning to her. She shuffled along with the rest, wondering what Peter expected to find in this place. They entered an open room, big and circular with many passages leading off from it. Overhead, a grate in the ceiling provided some daylight. Under it sat a large stone fountain, the carved sculpture of a sea nymph holding a jug, though no water poured from it, and the liquid in the basin was still. She stepped close enough to peer into the depths and noticed the gleam of coins.

"You going to make a wish?" Peter's hot breath brushed against the lobe of her ear.

She shrugged. "Why would I waste it when I don't need anything?" Not money. Or friends. She had a large extended family. The only thing she didn't have was...

A mate.

"Everyone wants something," he said, his breath still tickling her, his body framing her as he loomed behind her. If she turned, she'd be close enough to kiss him.

Wait, why would she want to kiss him?

He was a mission. Not a potential bedmate. No matter what her body and feline thought.

"Make a wish." His fingers pressed a coin into her hand. He aimed it over the water. "Ready, Nora. What do you want?"

As she let go of the coin, the only thing she could think of?

Peter.

Splash.

"What did you ask for?"

"If I tell you, it won't come true," was her light reply as she moved away from him and wandered the edges of the room, noticing the frescoes carved into the rock, the passageways leading off from the place. The sudden gurgling rush of water had Nora whirling to see the fountain had come to life, bubbling and gurgling, spitting water that held a strong mineral scent.

Had someone flipped a switch?

Given she'd been distracted, her gaze tracked the tourists. None of them interested in her. As for Peter…

Wait, where the hell was Peter?

She turned left and right, but he didn't appear. Impossible, he was just there. He must have slipped into one of the side passages.

She prowled the edge of the room, sniffing, noticing that his scent went past the one doorway blocked with a golden rope strung across it and marked by a sign with a big red circle slashed with a line. As she went to step over, someone grabbed her arm.

"You can't go there," the tour guide said.

"What's inside there?" she asked. Perhaps Peter went looking for a clue. She was kind of miffed he'd gone without her if that was the case.

Only the guide dashed that belief when he said, "It's simply another exit, but it's currently under construction and closed to the public."

An exit? Too late, she thought to check her fanny pack, the one Peter had pressed against, the one now missing a key.

Fucking Peter. He thought he could elude her.

She was about to show him his mistake.

CHAPTER SEVEN

Peter had escaped Nora with only a slight pang. Yeah, she'd probably get in trouble for losing him, but he couldn't have her around. There was something off about her. Also something hot and sexy. But mostly off.

The way she eyed him sometimes, her gaze taking on a glint, gave him a shiver. Her expression was smug, as if she hid something. The amusement as she laughed at him even as she thought to use him.

Threatened him.

Not happening. He wasn't some rube to be taken advantage of or distracted because of an attractive woman.

She'd been easier to dupe than expected, not questioning much the reason for their visit to the catacombs. Having played tourist there before, Peter had known it would get crowded around the fountain, the perfect chance to pickpocket—or in this case, retake—his key. He'd accidentally bumping into her, managing to slip it back into his possession. He'd done that kind of trick hundreds of times. What he didn't expect was the instant arousal the moment he got close or the twinge of guilt when he left her behind.

He'd not suffered at the hands of a certain old lady and her tiger to share the treasure now. If he wanted to put a spin on it, he could even claim he did this for Nora's own good because being around him would put her in danger.

Bad enough he'd worried the entire time he was on that cruise with his sister, wondering if he was safe. Nightmares of a stalking feline, wearing a pirate patch and somehow boarding the big ship, was a particularly vivid and ridiculous fear.

When his sister had told him the fake key had been passed on to someone else for investigation, he'd sighed in relief. Almost had a party when he found out the fake key was lost in a river. Good.

He'd assumed that would end the matter, but then Nora just had to follow him and find out the key they'd all been fighting over was a fake. How many people had she told? Did his enemies know yet? Those who commissioned its theft would want it, and a measure of his blood.

He really should try working for less criminal people. It would mean a pay cut. The rule followers had tight fists.

His distraction and fast-moving feet led him from the empty tunnel to a set of stairs that narrowed as they led upward. He emerged from the catacombs into a restricted area, cordoned off and dusty with workers in hardhats suddenly noticing his appearance and making a fuss.

"I think I'm lost!" he exclaimed, playing the American tourist. He let himself be quickly ushered out onto the street, where he blended with the crowd. He weaved quickly through the bodies, using them as cover should Nora be close by.

Only that shield suddenly dispersed—some people crying out in genuine annoyance, others with laughter —as the heavens opened up and the rain soaked everything.

Including him.

Ugh.

Sloshing in wet hikers wasn't his idea of fun. At least his backpack was waterproof. What it didn't have, because he'd not been able to bring one on the plane, was a weapon. Still, broad daylight in a mostly public place he should be fine, or so he told himself at the stomp of fast-moving feet. People probably trying to get to where they were going quickly.

Still, his pace increased, and he glanced over his shoulder. Stumbled as he saw the pair of big goons closing in on him.

He might have assumed it was a regular mugging if he'd not recognized the larger one with the shaven head and snarl. He worked for the people he'd screwed on the key.

Oh fuck. Both men had hands inside their coats. Would they shoot him in the street even with possible witnesses?

Forget any side alleys, he was staying in the public eye. He pounded through a puddle and did his best to go full speed over the uneven cobblestones. *Don't fucking fall.* If he twisted his ankle, he was done for.

His sprint slowed only slightly as he emerged into a plaza that had more traffic with people hustling packed strollers, covered in clear plastic tarps, while the parents and the walking germ vectors tucked under umbrellas. The majority of them appeared to be emerging from some gates, the wrought iron bars twisted into animal shapes. A zoo. A maze. A place to lose his pursuers.

Peter darted inside, hearing the yelling of the attendant that he hushed by flinging a bill. He ran, choosing a path at random, then another, leaving his pursuers behind. It helped that the rain fell thicker, a drenching curtain, rendering visibility difficult. What he really needed more than concealment was a way out that lost his pursuers. He wondered how they'd found him in the first place.

The reason hit him a second later.

His phone.

They must have hacked its location. He tossed it into the monkey enclosure, where furry paws gripped and began playing with it, the chattering and excitement high.

His sister would worry when she tried to call and didn't reach him, but he'd find public cafes and use a VPN to route messages to her so she didn't panic.

His steps slowed as he reached a fork. To the left was the aviary, to the right, big cats. Shudder.

Nope. He walked toward the bird section when he saw two bulky shapes far ahead.

Fucking seriously? His luck was utter shit.

Despite his dislike of the felines, Peter bolted in their direction, only to slip and fall on a slimy patch of melting ice cream. Chocolate goo amidst a squishy waffle cone. He hit the ground hard on one knee, and when he tried to stand, his leg threatened to buckle, the joint throbbing at the abuse.

He limped, losing speed. The pounding feet caught up. He turned to face his assailants, fists up, really wishing his first stop before the catacombs had been to a shop where he could have at least picked up a switchblade, something to defend himself other than feet and fists.

Still, he wasn't a slouch when it came to fighting, and the rain made aiming at him with a weapon difficult, as it bogged down the darts Baldy fired. Since he couldn't risk getting hit, he ran for the guys with a loud yell. The surprise worked to his advantage, and he slammed into Baldy's midsection before he could reload. They hit the ground with Peter on top, meaning he got in a few good pummels before the guy's buddy yanked him off.

Shorty, whom he should have named Brick because he looked like his face had hit one too many, raised a fist and offered a gap-toothed grin.

Peter kicked him in the midsection then swung a fist while Shorty was distracted. It connected, but before he could recover, arms wrapped around him from behind.

He thrashed, but Baldy was at least a foot bigger and many pounds larger. He lifted Peter off the ground and crushed him until he went still. Then he held him in front of Shorty, who had lost another tooth. It whistled moistly as he asked, "Where's the key?"

"What key?"

Shorty slammed a fist in his face.

"Ow." He played it up as if he were dying. Being stoic only got a person beaten harder.

"Where's the key?" Shorty asked again.

"Lost in a river."

"You're lying!" Baldy squeezed and shook until Peter gasped for air.

"Where is the key?" Shorty held his fist in front of Peter's face.

"Up yours." He lifted his feet and kicked. Shorty went tumbling, and Peter used that pushing momentum to snap free from Baldy. He hit the ground and rose swinging.

But two against one meant he couldn't avoid the beating. He knew enough to raise his arms to protect his head. Still, the punches rang in his ears. Clacked his teeth. A solid blow to his midsection sent him to the ground, where they kicked him in the ribs. By the time they searched him, he could only moan in pain, most of it real.

Shorty triumphantly said, "I've got the key!"

"Boss will be happy," the gruff Baldy replied. "We taking him back to the boss?"

Shorty nudged him with a foot. "No need since we got what we came for. Dump him in with the tigers. I hear he's got a thing for them." Followed by a snicker.

Peter almost whimpered. Not the fucking tigers. He kept his eyes closed against memories of the old lady. The feline. The way they both toyed with him in that basement until the lines of reality blurred.

The ground took a while to hit. The tigers were kept in a concrete bowl with sheer stone walls that they couldn't climb. He lay there for a moment, alive. Barely.

He hurt.

A lot.

The rain washed the blood away from his skin, but rather than help, it drew attention.

Chuff. Chuff. The hot, heated sound of an animal breathing. He cracked open an eye and immediately regretted it. A striped feline growled only paces away from him, crouched and ready to pounce. His death seemed certain.

And by a fucking tiger of all things.

Then shit got strange as a golden shape landed between him and the tiger. Four hairy legs and a swishing tail accompanied by a low warning snarl.

He blinked the rain out of his eyes, but it didn't change the fact a lion had appeared.

Great. Lions. Tigers. What was next, a bear?

Should he wait out the fight and hope he could take on a wounded victor before it ate him? Or draw both their notice and claws trying to escape?

Could he have option number three?

The tiger didn't like having its turf invaded and sprang first. The golden lion, with fur damp from the rain, met its leap and the bodies hit with a thud. They landed on their sides, and their feet were tangled as they clutched at each other, trying to chew off the other's face.

The battle didn't last very long. The tiger might have been larger, but the lion proved tricky and mean. It soon had the striped feline retreating to its den to lick its wounds.

The lion had won and would want to eat its prize.

He pushed against the ground, trying to lift himself, but sharp pain sent him lying flat, and breathing hard. He closed his eyes waiting for the tearing of claws or ripping of teeth to begin.

When nothing happened, he slitted one eye open to see the lion resting on its front paws, observing him. It even shook its head before huffing hotly on him.

Mocking the dumb human. Maybe if he played dead, it would leave him alone. He wouldn't be playing for long given his injuries were throbbing to the point he was wavering in and out of consciousness.

Which might have been why he could have sworn he heard Nora's voice snapping, "Stay in your corner, furball." Then more softly. "You idiot. You shouldn't have run."

CHAPTER EIGHT

"That will teach you to run away from me," was Nora's less than sympathetic response when he finally opened his eyes two days after she'd saved him in the tiger pit. He'd almost died. As it was, he wasn't in great shape.

"What happened?" He groaned.

At least he wasn't crying, which surprised her, given the extent of his injuries. She'd had to take him to an underground vet, who'd eyed the human she'd brought askance.

The verdict? Body bruised all over, with at least two broken ribs and a nose that might never sit straight again. Sexy.

"You had a bad day," she told him.

"Feels like I got hit by a truck," he grumbled. He

hissed as he moved, and she didn't help him. Let him suffer the consequences of his foolish actions.

He managed to sit up and lean against the headboard of the bed situated in the apartment she'd managed to score them. A nicer place than the shabby hotel of before.

"Care to explain why you were trying to feed yourself to the tiger?" she asked.

"I was tossed in there by the goons who stole my key."

"You mean the key you took from me?" she said too sweetly. It miffed her he'd managed to steal from her in the first place.

"Don't fucking start."

"Oh, I will fucking start because if you hadn't been so bloody stubborn and stupid you wouldn't have lost it and almost died."

"Trust me, given the way I'm hurting, I'm wishing I'd left it with you." His dark glare challenged her.

So she mocked him. "Yeah, you should have because I wouldn't have lost it." Yeah, she was rubbing salt in that wound. "Did you see who did this to you?"

"Pair of guys."

"Not helpful."

"Yeah, you know what else isn't helpful is you giving me attitude when what I need is fucking pain relief," he snapped.

"You wouldn't need anything at all if you'd not snuck off on me."

"Be glad I did, or you'd probably be in the same shape as me, or worse."

"Doubtful." It was never more evident how good shifter genes were than when looking at the human who was a mass of contusions that would take weeks to heal. Under normal circumstances.

She'd had to call on some Pride connections to get her hands on military-grade, top-secret salve to speed up the process. The ribs were already knitted together, although not solidly. That would take a while longer so he should avoid blows to the chest. His bruising had reached the yellow stage where it was almost gone. But the cure took a toll, sucking every ounce of energy from his body, leaving him with no body fat and muscles that would ache until he ate and rid himself of the dehydration.

"Do you have some acetaminophen? Something? Whiskey?" he asked, flexing his arm and clenching his fist as if trying to bring back circulation on a sleeping limb.

"No booze, but I do have electrolytes." Recommended by the vet. She tossed the bottle at him, but his currently slow reflexes meant it hit him in the stomach. He grimaced, and then it hit the floor.

"Oops." She felt bad and handed him an unmarked

bottle pulled from her back pocket. "Don't take too many, or you'll be catching little birdies and drooling."

He opened the jar and shook a pair of pills into his hand. He dry-swallowed them with a grimace.

She handed him the fluids. He chugged it and made an even bigger face. "The after-taste is ass."

"The correct answer is 'thank you for having this ready for me and for taking care of me while I was unconscious.'"

"How long was I out?"

"Two days."

He blinked at her. "Well fuck." He glanced at himself, the scrubs he wore, and turned red.

"I haven't been caring for you that entire time. The vet only released you to me a few hours ago."

"Vet?" He rubbed the bridge of his nose. "I think we need to back up a bit. Let's start with how you found me."

"Just followed my nose." She tapped it, knowing the truth would be the least likely thing he believed.

"More like followed my phone. I can't believe I was so stupid as to bring it along. Good news is it's gone now." He leaned back and closed his eyes.

"I guess that explains why your sister keeps texting me."

"You've heard from Charlie?"

"Every day, multiple times a day. Apparently,

when Arik said my mission with you was hush-hush, that didn't include her."

"Who is Arik?"

"No one." She blamed fatigue for her loose tongue. Two days of watching and worrying as the medically induced coma kept him in a state where the rapid healing wouldn't make him scream murder.

"Am I to understand you don't know my sister?"

"I do now. Speaking of whom, she'd love to hear from you." She handed him her phone, and he looked horrified.

"You idiot. Did you not hear what I said about being tracked via my phone? Get rid of it before they trace it to you. To me."

She snorted. "Not all of us were stupid enough to bring along an unsecured cellular device. For a criminal, you're not very criminally."

"Says the lady with black market tech in her hand."

"Is that jealousy I hear because my toys are better than yours?"

"Your bedside manner sucks," was his sulky reply.

"Don't make me get you some cheese for that whine."

"I'm allowed to complain. I almost died. By the way, how did you get me out of the tiger pen before those cats ate me?"

"Not easily. You're a heavy dude."

He snorted then winced. "As if you carried me out."

"You calling me a wimp?"

"I'm saying I outweigh you by at least forty or fifty pounds."

"And? It's all in the technique. Or is your arguing more because your chauvinistic ass can't handle a woman saved you?"

He made a moue of annoyance. "I'm injured. Must you turn all feminist on me?"

"Don't be a caveman and I won't have to. You could be a little more grateful considering I saved your ass."

"Thank you. I was in a bad spot."

"Not sure how much worse it could have gotten. It's a miracle you're alive."

"Would you believe a lion saved me?" Again, he tried to laugh, only to gasp in pain.

"You mean a lioness?" she couldn't help but huff indignantly. "Males have giant fluffy manes and are lazy as fuck. A male lion would have let you be eaten."

"Whatever. Boy kitty. Girl. Doesn't matter. It stopped that tiger from eating me."

Her fur bristled at the dismissive tone. "Maybe you should be a little more appreciative." A part of her wanted to press the point, wanted him to recognize she'd saved him at her own peril. She'd had no choice but to shift to save him from the tiger in the zoo. Then she'd shifted again to get him out of there. At the time, he'd been passed out and hadn't seen her. He hadn't made the correlation.

Yet. But if she wasn't careful, he would discover her secret, and then she'd have no choice.

Claim him. Her feline's suggestion was at odds with the prescribed death sentence for humans who knew too much.

"Guess now that the key is gone, you'll be taking off," he said, the pain pills having obviously kicked in as he swung his legs over the side of the bed.

"Is that what you're doing? Going home?"

"What else would I do?"

"I'm surprised you're giving up that easily." Disappointed too. She'd not taken him for a quitter.

"There is nothing easy about it. But without the key, there is no quest," was his angry retort.

"Wait, we are on a quest?" That sounded way better than the job she'd been handed so far.

"We were. Without the key, we're stuck."

"Says you. Way I see it we have two choices. Go after the people with the key and get it back, or get to the treasure before them."

"There is no we." He grunted as he stood and wavered on his feet.

"It's either we or me, and if it's just me, you should

know you'll spend that duration locked in this room. You decide." She arched a brow.

"And they call me the felon."

She smiled. "Is that a yes?"

"How is it you're blackmailing me but I don't hate you?"

"Because I'm cute." She grinned sassily at him.

"Sometimes. You're mostly persistent."

"Very. But I'll have you know I make a most excellent partner. Just ask Zach."

"Your boyfriend."

"Nope." She stepped close enough she had to look up to keep his gaze. "That was just an act. I am single. Available. And my favorite position is on my hands and knees." True. And a shocking admission. She almost blushed. But then she caught his reaction.

He sucked in a breath, swayed, and almost toppled.

She put a hand on his chest. "Careful, Montgomery."

"What happened to Peter?"

"Depends. Are we partners?"

"You keep wanting us to be equals, and yet I'm the one who knows where we need to go next."

"And I'm the one with the connections to get us there. I just need to know where so I can arrange transportation."

"First off, there will be no arranging of anything

because it's too easy for those goons to track if they're still watching me. And second, I'm not sure."

"Liar. You came to Europe for a reason."

"More like a hunch based on a riddle that I'm probably misinterpreting."

"You're referring to the story in that children's fairy tale book."

He eyed her sharply. "Have you seen it?"

"No, but I was briefed on it." AKA, Zach flipped quickly through the book retrieved in Peter's apartment so she could get the gist of the story via the images. "Basically, monster meets girl, goes on quest, uses a key to open some kind of chest. And they live happily ever after."

"In a nutshell, yes."

"We're going to find that treasure."

"Maybe. Keep in mind, even if it ever existed, it's probably long gone."

"Are you really going to play that game? You think it's real and that it's still there."

"I think this might be a wild goose chase. I mean think of it, a hidden treasure that can be found by following clues in a children's story?"

"But you believe it."

He shrugged. "I do, and yet it's crazy. I'm crazy. Like legit nut job. Just got out of a padded room a few weeks ago."

"Just because they called you insane doesn't make it true. Maybe they just didn't understand you."

That brought a choked chuckle from him. "Oh, they understood me all right. That was the whole problem."

"Why were you there?" The medical reports were in Russian and only had a summary paragraph in English that said he was convinced he was being hunted by an old lady and her tiger. The doctors claimed he'd suffered a psychotic break with reality.

But she saw it as a clue. Peter had seen something. And she was going to find out what.

If he stopped being stubborn.

"I was put there because they found me naked in the woods eating grubs."

"Raw, or did you cook them first to make them into crunchy protein bites?"

"This isn't fucking funny. My life isn't a joke."

"I was being serious. Personally, I like them cooked with a hint of salt and chili powder. The best are grasshoppers. The big kind. Very flavorful."

"There is something seriously wrong with you, Nora."

"Because I'm not caught up in the usual Western hang-ups when it comes to my sources of protein? Bugs are meat of a different kind."

"That's just wrong and just another reason why you and I should part ways."

He was trying to blow her off again so he could find the treasure by himself. Enough. Time he realized he wasn't the one calling the shots. "Since you're so desperate for me to leave, good luck getting anywhere. You have no identification. No money. Not even any pants." She glanced at his groin then back at him as she said, "Although you do have the goods to make a few bucks turning tricks."

His face turned red. "I'll call my sister."

"Go right ahead. Call her. Tell her where you are. Even better, maybe I will and tell her to come save you herself."

"You wouldn't dare!" he growled.

"You're right, I wouldn't, but you will because, without me, you're stuck. Have fun." She rose and made as if to leave.

"Don't."

"Don't what?"

"Don't go."

"Why?"

He glared at her. "You know why."

She smirked. "Say it, Peter. Say you need me."

"I. Need. You." Spoken through gritted teeth, and yet her inner feline practically purred.

"Was that so hard?" Her gaze dropped, and the

more she stared, the more she noticed not all parts of him hurt. "I see that it is. *Hard,*" she purred.

His embarrassment had him flushing, but he recovered enough to say, "Since you're good at fixing stuff, feel free to fix it."

"Maybe I will." She winked. "You and I are going to have a grand adventure."

"If we survive. Even though my enemies got their hands on the key, if they find out I'm alive, they might come after me."

"Yay." She clapped her hands. "I love a challenge. Don't you?"

He eyed her and shook his head. "There is something seriously wrong with you."

"I prefer to think of it as seriously right. Now, let's discuss this supposed treasure. According to my briefing, the story claims it's some kind of magical spell to turn a monster into a human. Sounds fascinating."

He snorted. "And obviously not true. That kind of magic doesn't exist."

She arched a brow. "If you don't believe, then why are you chasing after it?"

"For the same reason archeologists look for tombs and mummies."

"Gold!"

He shook his head. "Wrong again. The true value will be in its history. The age of it. The fact it's unique. I have buyers who will pay big bucks to get their hands on whatever it is just to claim they own it."

"You're just going to sell whatever we find to the highest bidder?"

"What else would I do with it?"

What else indeed... "What if I told you I knew someone who would pay you enough you could retire richly for life."

"I'd say, how much?"

She quoted a ridiculous number that in the grand scheme of the Pride's finances wasn't all that much.

His eyes widened. "That would work if you're not shitting me."

"How about I give you a third now, as a measure of good faith. Then the rest when you help us find it."

"What if we can't or it's gone?"

"You still keep that third."

He thought about it for a moment. Then nodded. "Deal."

"Awesome. I guess the next step is arranging a flight. Where to, partner?"

"Only once I see the money."

He wouldn't budge on that point. Meaning, she had to bring him a disposable phone with data access, which he could use to verify she'd indeed deposited the money into his account. Only then did he show her the encrypted images of the book stored in the cloud Melly still couldn't access.

Nora scrolled through the images, unable to read the text but able to follow along looking at the pictures. It helped that he gave her an abbreviated version of the tale.

By the time they finished the story, which he'd had translated in pieces that he meshed together, she found herself pensive.

Also slightly shocked. It took her a moment to say, "The story in your book is slightly different than the one I heard about."

"Because there are several versions in circulation."

Which made her wonder which one was true, because, in Peter's copy, instead of the questing monster being turned into a man, the tsarina became a beast.

CHAPTER NINE

"There are two versions of the story?" Nora blinked in surprise.

"Yeah." Actually, more than two, according to his research.

"How is it you know about them? How did you even come across the book at all?"

"By accident." At her inquiring gaze, Peter explained. "I learned about it because of a job." He launched into the tale, because after all, why not?

It helped she listened raptly, and maybe it was time to remove some of the secrecy around it. After all, if he was going to die, someone should know the truth.

"I was actually playing it straight at the time. Working as a bartender at night, taking welding classes by day." What he didn't add was that life sucked. It consisted of work, study, sleep.

"Sounds like you were busy."

"My sister kept telling me it would be worth the effort. Nagged about the fact I was well past the age I should have smartened up and settled down." It should be noted, he didn't have a problem living the criminal life. It was the cops and his sister that interfered with it.

"Ugh. You too? I swear since my sisters all got married and pregnant that's all I hear. Christmas holidays. 'When you gonna get engaged?' New Year's. 'Single again?'" She grimaced.

"You don't want a boyfriend?"

"Are you applying?"

"No." Although he was attracted to her. Problem being, he had no idea if it was reciprocated. It would really be easier if girls got boners so boys could tell.

"Good because I like being single. I never want to settle down. Diapers and dishes. Staying home and being blah." She expressed his sentiments exactly.

"Right? Like I know some people love the whole 'let's stay home and raise a family together' shit, but personally, I'd rather run a fun con or smuggle in some crab."

"You've smuggled shellfish?" She blinked at him.

"Once. Those bastards are creepy at night." Not to mention, he would have sworn he'd seen faces in the waves when the boat docked with its illegal load. Feminine with flowing hair and beckoning smiles.

"I see the file I read on you only listed some of your talents."

Wait, she'd read a file? "What else did it say?"

"Wouldn't you like to know?" Her gaze dropped to a spot below his buckle, and he might have shifted, more to hide his growing erection.

Damn but the woman affected him. Every fucking time she walked into a room, his hormones ran wild.

"I thought you wanted to know about the two books I found."

"Please, tell me more." She waved a hand, her graciousness giving him permission to speak.

"An old friend approached me at work and said he knew of someone looking for a man with my skills for a job."

"And you said yes."

"Yeah." Despite knowing his sister would be pissed. "I couldn't resist. Going after the book wasn't just about the money."

"But also the adventure." She nodded. "I get it. Why do you think I love my job?"

"What exactly is your job?"

"Pretty much anything I want. Sometimes it's espionage. Acquisition. A few on grand scales," she boasted. "I've bodyguarded and kidnapped."

"Wait, kidnapped?"

"Don't worry. They deserved it."

Which didn't explain shit but did make him see her in a different light. "Ever killed someone?" he asked.

"Have you?" she countered.

"Only once. When I was doing time. It was shank or be shanked."

"You got caught. That's sloppy."

"That's my luck."

"I'd say your luck is pretty good if you only got caught once."

"It's been close a few times." Too close. More reason why he should retire, and yet he couldn't leave the adrenaline behind. The beating he'd suffered was already fading in memory, meaning he'd probably act stupid again.

"So the book," she said, drawing him back to the present. "You were hired to find it. Meaning someone knew it existed and what it contained."

As the painkillers kicked in, he found it easier to move and began craving food. Did this apartment have a stocked kitchen? He shuffled toward the door. "Obviously someone knew it existed or they wouldn't have hired my services, but I never met the buyer. In my line of work, it's rare to meet a client. They like to keep a layer of deniability in place."

"How did you track down the book?"

"More like the client did and sent me in to fetch it. The job consisted of an address and description. A tome bound in black leather, tooled in gold leaf. Inside, an illustrated story. Old." The job? Crack the safe where it was being hidden and bring it back for a plump reward.

It proved ridiculously easy to get inside given the target's teenage daughter left the side gate unlocked every night for her boyfriend. She also deactivated the alarm system on the house.

No one noticed the extra shadow that entered the mansion. Not a single creak gave away his presence as he made it to the massive study. The painting on the wall proved light and easy to remove, revealing an embedded safe, old-school style, with a dial and everything. His favorite kind. He pressed his ear to the metal and listened, but the stupid fish tank in the office with its gurgling made it difficult and he couldn't just blow the door off.

"You're a safe cracker!" Nora breathed as if in wonderment, having listened with rapt attention to his story. "That's cool."

"I have a knack for locks." He downplayed his innate skill. "It's not a big deal. Mostly you need quiet. Pure quiet." Which was why he had unplugged the fish tank then rested his ear on that big beauty of a safe.

He closed his eyes to the outside world and tuned inwards. *Click. Tick. Crank. Tock.*

He didn't even realize he'd relaxed into that happy Zen place until she said, "You love cracking safes."

"I do. It's satisfying."

"Can you unlock electronic ones too?"

"Yeah, but it doesn't have the same feel."

"If we get a chance, would you show me how it's done?"

Show her? He must have looked surprised because she ducked her chin, for the first time acting as if shy. "I'd like to learn."

"Sure." He'd never taught anyone. Would have laughed at the idea until she asked. Now he couldn't think of anything he'd like to do more.

"So what did you find inside?"

"Books. In the plural. Which I wasn't expecting. It didn't help they looked identical."

Which one did they want? Did they even realize there was another?

Pulling them out, he'd run his hands over them, the first feeling as it should, grainy and musty smelling. The other...it held a hint of cold to it, as if it had sat in a fridge.

He shivered as he opened it. Could swear he felt a cold breeze.

"Since I didn't know which was the right one, I

tucked them both into my satchel. But only handed over one of them. Never said a word about the other."

"I'd have done the same thing. How did you choose which one to keep?"

He wasn't about to say one of them almost made him tingle. That was just weird, so he stuck to, "I liked the one with the unconventional ending."

"Did the people who hired you ever find out about the other book?"

He shook his head. "Nope. Not that I know of. And like I said, it seems like there might be a few versions in circulation."

"So when did you go after the key?"

"I didn't until they hired me. I was staying low with the book just in case. My plan was to eventually auction it on the dark net." Not the whole truth.

He'd gone back to bartending, but on his breaks, he tried to decipher the text in the book, enlarging the pictures he'd taken and doing searches to see what language it was in. When the mighty Google didn't recognize it, he knew he was on to something. Something big.

"I'm surprised you're admitting this to me," Nora said, interrupting his mental memory. "Aren't you afraid I'll rat you out for stealing?"

He snorted. "As if you always obey the laws."

"Do I look like a criminal to you?"

"Bad girl, definitely."

She tossed her hair. "Thank you."

"Not going to deny you're a rule breaker?"

"Sometimes they get in the way." Her tiny smile was too fucking cute.

He looked away and went back to his story. "You want to know about the key."

"First tell me more about the book. You didn't sell it. You had it translated."

She was astute. "I did. After all, a good salesman should know his product. After much research, I discovered it was an unused medieval Russian dialect only taught by one professor."

"And rather than email someone in Russia for a translation, you traveled there to meet with him?"

"Yes. For two reasons. The same people who hired me to find the book were already looking for the key. They had a head start."

"But you found it."

"Actually, they did. They hired me to go get it for them."

"But you never handed it over."

"The moment they asked, I planned a way to keep it for myself. That's when I had the fake made based off the images in the book. I managed to acquire the real one and had the copy ready to hand off when I was..." How to summarize his next terrifying moments? "Detained."

"You disappeared, and your buyers didn't get any key. What's surprising is they didn't tear apart your place right then and there. The reports say your sister lived in your place for months before anyone thought to dismantle it looking for the missing key."

"They probably thought I had it with me." Because he knew for a fact they'd been looking for him. Watched his sister for months before acting to threaten her, hoping to use her to flush him out.

It wouldn't have worked given he was still catching birdies in the mental institution. A fancy word for an old drafty building with wards kept docile via the administration of drugs.

"Were you hiding for those six months?"

"Not so much hiding as detained."

"By the asylum. But what about the weeks before that? Where were you?"

In the grips of pure evil? Too much? He stuck to, "Being held prisoner by someone with an axe to grind."

"Who?"

"The original owner of the key. Only she was more annoyed I'd escaped her and her pet tiger than the actual theft."

"Wait, so the tiger and shit you kept talking about was real?"

"Parts of it were, like the bit where she locked me up and hurt me to amuse her pet."

Distaste crossed her features. "That's sick! I'm going to need the name of that lady."

"I'm afraid it won't do you much good. She's disappeared. It's believed the tiger they found in her house might have eaten her."

"Happens when they get old," was her odd reply. "So the old lady tortured you until you escaped. Then what?"

"I lived like an animal in the woods for a while until they found me and put me in the loony bin. Pumped me full of drugs on account I wouldn't stop talking about the tiger. That's where Lawrence found me."

"Meanwhile, the people who hired you got desperate to get their hands on the key. What I don't get is, shouldn't they have believed the one lost in the river was the only copy?"

Nora was well informed. He shrugged. "I don't know why their sudden interest again."

"Somehow they figured out it was a fake. Which makes me wonder if they know the book you gave them is different than the one you kept."

"Only subtly," he stated. "Slight variations in the wording."

"Such as the tsarina becoming the beast instead of vice versa."

"Which is just as dumb as the other version I've heard of where the monster turns into a man."

"You don't think it's possible?" she asked as if utterly serious.

He couldn't help but scoff. "Werewolves aren't real. It's just physically impossible."

"And yet don't skinwalkers exist in just about every culture in legend?"

"Doesn't make it real. In olden days they also used to think the sun and moon only rose because of the gods. That sacrifices could make for a good crop."

"There are things in this world that would seem fantastical to people only a century ago. Look at technology and its evolution."

"Technology is built. Biology is static."

She laughed, as if that were the funniest thing ever. "For a man who believes in a treasure quest, you're awfully rigid on other matters."

"I'll admit I don't know if that book and the key lead to anything. Probably fool's gold, but..." He shrugged. What if he could hit the jackpot? The score of all scores. Even if he didn't, the adventure itself still appealed.

"If we assume the book and its story are clues, then we can replicate the hero's journey so long as we find the starting point. Which would be here." She found the image she wanted and pointed. "Some kind of place with sandy dunes where we have to enter the mouse's lair to find the path to the icy field." She kept flipping, but he jolted forward.

"Wait, what did you say? Go back a page."

"Why? Did you see something?" She flipped to the previous image, the white and silver illustration glinting bright.

"You called that an ice field." He pointed.

"What else would it be?"

"The book refers to it as the land of diamonds. For some reason, I took it literally. I've been trying to find a way to check out some of the mines located in Russia without getting shot for trespassing. I never even thought it might be ice."

"The advantage of not being too close to the story," she quipped. "Which leads me to ask, what makes you think the treasure is in Russia?"

"Where else would it be?"

"Somewhere tropical for starters given it starts on a beach." She pointed to the early image of dunes by an edge of water.

"Siberia has those kinds of sandy hills."

"Sounds like you might be stretching. Especially since the last location clue is a volcano with a tunnel. Still sounds more tropical to me."

"Except there are volcanoes in Russia, like the ones by the Kamchatka Peninsula."

"I guess it's possible." She chewed her lower lip. "But what if you're wrong and we go off in the wrong direction?"

His stomach dropped. "We'll never get the key back or beat them to the treasure."

"You said we." She grinned. "Finally ready to admit you need me?"

"I need the reward I'll get for solving this thing."

"How sure are you? Ready to put your money where your mouth is?"

"Meaning?"

"If you're wrong, and it's not in Russia, you don't get any more money."

Wager on a hunch? He held out his hand. "It's a bet."

CHAPTER TEN

"So where to first?" Nora asked.

"A part of me wants to just go looking for that final volcano, but..." Peter trailed off and shrugged, his expression sheepish.

"I get it. In the book, the hero has to do the quest in order, or he'll never find it." She laughed. "Guess if we're going to do this, we should do it right. First stop, the sand dunes in Siberia."

Since she seemed keen on booking their trip, he let her handle it and was glad of it. It meant first class flights into the heart of Russia. Once there, she hustled them off to the train station where they got not just a private cabin but all the bells and whistles.

He sat down on the plush seating and sighed. "This is the life."

"Might as well travel in style, given we could have to rough it at a moment's notice," she stated.

"What is the plan once we get to the next station? Are we riding into the desert?"

"You'll see. It's a surprise." Scarier words had never been heard.

Then again, he didn't get the impression she expected to rough it much. His knapsack of supplies held more than her satchel did. She liked to travel light, or so she claimed. She had also boasted, *"I'm a most excellent hunter and can easily live off the land."*

"I'd rather sleep in a bed," had been his grumbled reply. True and false at the same time. He did enjoy his creature comforts, but he also loved the exhilaration of a quest. Of setting out to solve a mystery. To locate a treasure. To outsmart everyone else.

"I imagine the dunes have shifted since the book was written," he said as they waited for their trip to begin.

She held out her phone on a selfie stick, oddly enough, aiming it at their window. Doing what? Was she videotaping the station outside? Should he remind her about not posting to social media?

"If the treasure was easy to find, then it's already gone. We have to assume it's not."

"Surely we're not the first to try." The closer they

got, the more worried he was they'd gone on a possible wild goose chase.

"According to the book, you have to use the key to get the treasure."

"We don't have the key."

"Yet. You're a professional thief. Steal it back."

She said it as if it were simple. And it might be if they could catch up to the goons who took it.

"We don't even know if it's the right key." He ignored his gut that said it was.

"It's the only key we know about, though. Despite looking deep, Melly hasn't found shit except for another knock-off copy of the fairy tale, but in that version, the hero dies before he can get the treasure and the heroine throws herself off a balcony."

"That's a Brothers Grimm kind of ending."

"I like it!" was her dark reply that had him laughing. "We're in the process of acquiring it to compare against the version you left behind."

"I wonder why all the differences," he mused aloud.

"Only the ending seems to change. In other respects, they are almost the same. The quest. The location. Just the outcome shifts based on small things."

"It's the little things that usually get you in the end. Such as the mouse in the first clue."

"Surely it can't be that hard to find a mouse in the desert," she said.

"You going to follow every single rodent you locate?" Did she hear the inanity of it?

"What's your plan then?"

"The following of the mouse is more symbolic. In other words, he sees something living and travels to it, leading him out of the desert and into the ice fields. Which obviously don't exist since there aren't any bordering the Siberian dunes."

"If you don't believe in the mouse, then does that mean I can have them for breakfast?"

Since she was the woman who had admitted to eating bugs, he feared she wasn't joking. "Do you scramble chunks with your eggs?"

"Now you're just being weird. They make great stock for an all-day simmering stew. Start at breakfast and it's ready by dinner."

"That's nasty."

"Only if you don't rinse them first."

He had no reply to that. None. "I'll stick to my Mini-Wheats in the morning and nachos at night I think."

"It's a good thing I've seen you eat meat, or I'd start getting worried I was traveling with an herbivore."

"The horror," he mocked.

"Seriously. The vegan movement worries me. Why

would anyone ever want meatless meat? It's just wrong. So wrong," she lamented.

"Spoken like a true carnivore."

"You have no idea," she muttered low enough he almost didn't hear it.

The train lurched into motion, and she finally pulled her selfie stick close enough to replay her video.

"What were you taping?"

"People boarding after us. I recorded it to a cloud where Melly can run it and see what our facial recognition program picks up."

The reply stumped him for a second. "You use facial rec?" That was high-end shit.

"We have all kinds of tools. Remember that next time you try to run." She tapped the screen on her phone and swiped. Had she seen something?

"Do you think someone followed us?"

"If those hired to find you are half decent at what they do, then yes. After all, they've been pretty accurate as to where and when to hit so far."

"A little too accurate. I'm beginning to wonder if maybe my sister's hubby is trying to get rid of me." Because she was the only person he'd talked to. While he knew she wouldn't betray him, he couldn't vouch the same for Lawrence. That man had secrets and a side he'd wager Charlie didn't know about. A dark side.

"If he wanted to get rid of you, he'd do it himself. Lawrence isn't a pussy that way."

"Know him well, do you?" he almost snarled, only to realize at the last second his anger stemmed from jealousy.

"Since I was a kid. He's a cousin of a cousin."

"And is Lawrence the one calling the shots?" He still didn't have a clear idea of who Nora worked for.

"He's not my boss."

"But your boss is the one buying the treasure if we find it?"

"Aren't you just curious like a cat? That's enough questions for now. We should get some sleep. Big day coming up." Then she proceeded to do just that, leaning back in her seat with her eyes closed.

Peter did his best to join her, but as if landing back in Russia were a trigger, every time he closed his eyes, he was back in that basement. Dug into the very ground itself, the walls were braced by wood and concrete blocks. The floor was pure dirt and rock.

Irina—an old lady who'd somehow managed to kidnap a full-grown man—kept him in that basement, locked in a cage. Too short to stand. Barely wide enough to lie down.

She took his clothes. His identity. She didn't speak to him in English, and no amount of pleading aided his cause. She'd come with a plate of food in the morning, noon, and night. Hosed him off with freezing cold water at her whim.

He hated the icy showers because they were the prelude to the true horror.

Irina would clomp up those wooden steps, leaving his cage unlocked. The first time, he was filled with such hope. He'd exited those bars and run for the nearest basement window. Nailed shut, and even if he could break the glass, the bars were too skinny for him to wiggle through.

And that was when he heard the basement door open. She must have remembered she forgot to lock him in. Surely, he could overpower one little old lady. He ran for the stairs, only to skid to a stop.

He'd have sworn the tiger on the steps grinned at him. By the time he crawled, sobbing, into his cage, trying to escape teeth, claws, and, worst of all, that raspy tongue, he was half dead.

Irina nursed his wounds, and two days later, out came the hose again. Followed by her pet tiger. Repeat.

Until he finally tricked the old lady. She'd come down and put his plate on the floor. He didn't move. When she returned at lunch, his meal was untouched. He lay in the same spot.

She sniffed at him. Poked him with her cane. He didn't move. Didn't flinch when she jabbed harder.

She muttered something in Russian before opening

the cage. He hoped she wouldn't hear his thumping pulse.

She reached for him, and he moved, shoving his shoulder into her, pushing her off balance. Then he scurried for the open door and slammed it shut behind him.

Locked it. Faced the old lady, whose eyes glowed with fury. And when she snarled, her huge teeth reminded him of another set.

He fled. Ran like a wild thing into the woods, flinching at every scrape of a branch, expecting claws. Whimpering when he thought he saw striped fur between leaves.

The shame of his terror startled him awake, and he caught Nora watching him.

"You having a nightmare?"

"Was it the screaming that gave it away?" He couldn't help the sarcasm.

"What was it about?"

"Nothing."

"The nothing you claim you don't remember?" she asked, a little too astute.

"Why do you care?"

"I don't. I'm curious. You obviously remember more than you claim."

"I'd rather not. You've seen my scars."

"And? You healed."

He eyed her. "It hurt." That seemed obvious to him.

She snorted. "So do a lot of things. You have nightmares about all your boo-boos?"

How dare she downplay his trauma? "I almost died."

"But didn't. You going to be a drama llama about it the rest of your life?"

"You're annoying," he growled.

"So tell me to shut up."

"Shut up."

"Make me," she said with a smirk.

There was only one way he could think of that might actually work. Before he could tell himself it was a bad idea, he leaned forward and kissed her.

He meant to give her a quick peck, enough to shock her into silence, only the light embrace turned into a lingering touch that resulted in him kneeling in front of her. Her hands cupped his face, devouring his mouth. Their tongues got involved. Their breathing turned erratic, and next thing he knew his hands were up her shirt, cupping her breasts, rubbing thumbs over her nipples.

He shoved up her shirt and let his mouth follow where his fingers dared, sucking at the nipple through her bra. In the back of his mind, a part of him screamed he was acting irrational. But there wasn't enough blood left in his head to care.

She was the one to wiggle her pants down enough she could kick them off and then spread her legs for him. Short, golden curls tight to her mound, lithe thighs, and glistening pink goodness.

It was wild and crazy. He pushed her legs so that her knees were bent, her heels on the seat, exposing her to him. He took full advantage, lapping at her, tasting her honeyed sweetness, loving how she panted as he flicked her swollen nub. He groaned when she grabbed his hair and hissed, "Finger me while you lick."

With pleasure. One finger, two, he made it really tight with three, feeling her clench around him, her hips bouncing a bit in time to the strokes of his tongue. The spasm as she came had him moaning.

She rode his hand, her climax an ongoing ripple that had her gasping, "Yes, yes, now fuck me."

Oh, hell yes, he wanted to fuck her. He rose on his knees, unbuckled his pants. His hard dick sprang forward, ready to bury itself, when there was a knock.

He ignored it and rubbed the tip of his dick against her.

But she wasn't eying him with passion anymore. Instead, she eyed the door.

The handle to their locked compartment rattled.

What the fuck? He stood and tucked himself back

in as she scrambled into her pants. There was a thud against the door.

"Someone's trying to get in." He couldn't help his incredulous note.

"Guess we were followed after all."

"What do we do?" Because their options seemed limited to two things—hope they didn't break open the door, or take them out first. He rummaged in his knapsack for a knife, whereas Nora slung her satchel on and stood by the window.

Thump.

"Why the fuck are they still chasing us?" he muttered.

"Get your stuff together. We're leaving."

A good idea. He stuffed his coat into the knapsack and put on his shoes. Only to then wonder where they were going. The train was still moving. To exit they'd have to get past the person knocking.

Thud.

The train slowed, and he swayed on his feet. They must be hitting a curve.

"This is where we get off," Nora announced.

He would have questioned, but she smashed the window. Like literally took it out. The cabin filled with a cold, brisk wind as the train kept hurtling down the tracks.

"We can't jump off," he yelled even as the door rattled some more.

"You got a better idea?" Nora stood framed by the window.

Outside it was dark, meaning he could only imagine the countryside flying by. He felt the chill bite of the air and wondered if he was insane.

And then remembered that, according to the doctors, he was.

"Any advice on not dying?" he asked as he heaved himself from the door and dove for the window.

"Tuck and roll."

CHAPTER ELEVEN

Being a cat, Nora landed on two feet with a run that slowed. While her human partner hit the ground with his shoulder and then tumbled before stopping face first on the ground.

"Ugh," his clumsy carcass groaned.

"You're alive!" she declared in case he wasn't sure.

"Why can't I have a normal life?" Peter rolled onto his back then heaved to his knees. "Fuck me, I am getting too old for this. Let's move before they come after us."

"Good news. No one's following."

"While I like your optimism, they probably jumped too." He grimaced as he rolled his joints, and she hoped he'd not busted his newly fixed ribs.

"I didn't pay him enough to do that." The truth slipped out.

It didn't go unnoticed by Peter. "Wait a second. What do you mean 'pay'?"

"Well, I had a feeling you might balk at the whole jumping off a train at night thing, so I hired some incentive."

"You faked an attack to get me to leap? You're fucking crazy," he yelled. "I could have died. Or broken something."

"But didn't. I chose the spot where the train always slows for a curve, and look, soft, sandy landing." She nudged the ground with her shoe.

"Soft for who?" was his incredulous reply.

"I didn't have any problem." The surefire thing to rile a man's pride.

"Because I swear, you're part cat."

"Fifty-fifty at least," she said, knowing he'd think she jested.

He brushed himself off. "You should have just told me your plan instead of lying about it."

"Don't be so grouchy. I get it, you're feeling a little blue balled. Not my fault you have the worst timing when it comes to making a move on me. I mean, five minutes sooner and we would have been done. Heck, depending on your speed, it might have been less."

"I— Fuck! You... Jeezus. Goddamn." He kept muttering as he stalked away from her.

"Don't be mad," she called after him.

"I'm not mad."

"Would you feel better if we had sex right now?" she offered and was ready to strip down if needed to help him vent his frustration.

"No."

"Now that's a lie," she stated as she caught up. "We both know coming feels good."

"Maybe I don't want to come with you."

"Who else you going to come for? Hunh?" Oops. A little jealousy spilled out.

"My hand if that's all that's available." He kept stomping.

She followed, letting him work off his anger. Maybe she shouldn't have hidden her plan from him and instead treated him like an equal. Problem being they weren't equal. She could literally break him in half. She might also have to kill him if he posed a threat to the Pride.

Mate him.

Her damned feline had one solution to fix it all. The one thing she wouldn't do. Get tied down. Ugh. No. Never.

As they went over their first hump of sand, the starlight and moon gave them enough illumination to see the dunes, but no water. "Since you seem to be marching with purpose, I assume you know where you're going," Nora hollered.

"Nope. And neither did the hero." Whose name she'd yet to actually discover. Probably something unpronounceable.

"There was water in the picture. Maybe we should look for that."

"What if the climate shift or another natural event wiped it out?" He cast her a glance. "I've been studying the maps. Trying to find a way the route makes any sense. But the dunes don't connect to ice. and the ice isn't touching the volcanoes."

"Does the journey have to make sense?"

"Yes, because it doesn't take him weeks to travel to them all."

"Maybe he had a fast horse."

"And we're wandering around on foot." He paused and eyed her, hands on his hips. Lips pinched. Frame taut with anger. "What were you thinking exactly when you decided we should leap out into the wild unknown with hardly any supplies?"

"That we would find a mouse and follow it."

He stared at her. Said nothing for a second. Just stared.

"What? It's in the book."

"Any mouse is probably long dead."

"Unless it can live eternally or have children passing on the torch." She had a reply for everything.

"You do realize you are literally talking about

finding a mouse. To show us a secret passage. Fuck me." He rubbed his face. "What was I thinking? This is nuts."

"But fun," she stated as she finally drew level with him. "Maybe we won't find a thing. Does it really matter when getting there is the best part?"

"You're different than other people in how you see things."

"I am." No point in denying it.

"You had us jump off a moving train to hike in the desert."

"I did."

"You do realize that kind of crazy shit really should be done only if high on acid."

"I'm sure we could find something we could smoke." The effects weren't long-lived for a shifter, but it could be done.

"Probably not the best idea given we have limited munchies. I'd rather find somewhere warm to hunker for the night." He rummaged in his bag and pulled out his coat then cursed. "My fucking gloves are on the train."

"You shouldn't have strewn your stuff everywhere."

"You should have told me I wouldn't have time to check for loose ends." He glared right back.

She grinned. "If they get cold, let me know. I have somewhere warm you can stick them."

His expression...oh it was sultry deliciousness. She couldn't help but kiss him. Quickly, because they really shouldn't spend too much time in this place forbidden to the Pride. Something about a treaty. Could cause a diplomatic shifter issue. Blah blah.

"If it gets any colder, we could be in trouble," he noted.

"We could always dig a burrow and snuggle for heat."

"I am not earth-worming it for the night."

"Then we walk."

He sighed. "You couldn't have had some dirt bikes tossed off by your hired goon?"

"Want me to play you a violin?"

Rather than reply, he bundled as best he could, and then he removed a layer and made her wear it despite her protests, apparently not liking the thickness of her garments. She didn't need it but had to admit his worry for her was cute.

They moved off, the night wind brisk and whipping small grains of sand. Even she could admit it wasn't pleasant walking. But she kept that to herself.

A few dunes later, she couldn't help but notice his frosting breath, his hands tucked into his sleeves. She'd not accounted for the fact he didn't stay as warm as her.

The rocky outcrop partially buried by sand proved a perfect spot to say, "Why don't we shelter here for a bit and warm up."

"I like that plan," he huffed, dumping his pack in the sheltered vee of the stones. He pulled out a can and lit it. By the light of it, she could read the label. Camping Fire in a Can. To the point and practical in a place with no wood. Also, very nerdy.

"You remembered to bring gel to burn but not a spare set of gloves?" she said.

"I had gloves. I was a little distracted."

Yeah. Distracted by her. The headiness went to the spot between her legs.

The tingle she'd felt on and off since he'd made her come returned. She wished they could have had a few more minutes on that train. That they had the time now. Alas, duty called.

"I'm going to look around. Back in a few minutes."

Still crouching, he reached to grab her ankle. "Stay here. We shouldn't split up. You might not find me again in the dark."

"I'd find you. I'll follow my nose."

"Great to know I stink that bad," he drawled.

"How about I just follow the light back so don't snuff it."

"Maybe you should take it with you?" he offered.

"No thanks. Because then you'd see what I was really doing because that was me trying to delicately say I need to tinkle." Not entirely a lie.

"Oh. I kind of do too. Maybe I should go out there."

"Stop being so dramatic. You pee on the other side of the rock, and I'll just go over there by that hump for a squat."

"Bring the fire with you."

"No. Can you stop with the caveman routine? Just because I don't swing a dick doesn't mean I'm scared of the dark."

"Just trying to be fucking nice," he grouched.

"Nice would be resuming what we started," she quipped.

Dead silence.

Good silence or the bad kind? She kind of wanted to know, only she didn't have time because she'd caught a scent. Something different that didn't belong. Rank, and a bit of rot. It had been downwind until the slight breeze shifted.

She walked quietly, her senses tuned. She would have preferred switching to her lion. However, with Peter nearby, she had to be careful.

The sandy ground molded to each step she took and made it hard to focus her gaze on any one spot given the undulations, the ripples, and peaks.

It hid until she was almost upon it. The monster rose suddenly, a fake heap come to life, and hissed.

What the fuck was it?

The thing, with its rat-like body, had a long tail, barbed at the end, and tan-colored fur blotching parts of its body. Other sections were pasty wrinkly skin.

It stood on two legs, its front paws tipped with knife-long—and she'd bet sharp—claws. The fetid stench coming off it was enough to make her want to gag and this from someone who'd tracked dead bodies in the past.

The only thing that wasn't scary about it?

Its size. It didn't even reach her knee. Nora dove close and grabbed it by the scruff. It let out a god-awful squeal that drew Peter with a cry.

"Nora! Are you okay?"

She carried her prize back with a triumphant, "I think I found the mouse."

"What?" Holding the gel can, Peter got close enough to see what she caught. "What the fuck is that?" He visibly recoiled while her captive monster hissed, its stubby whiskers twitching.

"This is our next clue," she stated, stopping a few feet from Peter, holding the thrashing creature firmly.

It really wasn't cooperating, and it squealed something fierce.

"Listen Ms. Mutant Rodent Wrangler, I think you should put that thing down before you catch something."

"I will let go when you're ready to follow it."

"I am not following that creature." His nose wrinkled.

"We have to. It's the mouse."

"It's a freak of nature."

"Ah, don't say that about the baby."

"That baby is two feet tall instead of a few inches."

"Makes you wonder how big the adults get," she replied as the monster calmed and hung in her grip.

"Wait," he said slowly, and she could see the gears in his head working. "If that's a baby then—"

The sand erupted in a geyser as Mommy—with her numerous hanging teats—erupted from the ground. Like its progeny, it had ragged fur with patches of slime oozing from sores. One jagged horn curled from beside a rounded ear, a tusk on one side of its massive, gaping maw. And one pissed-off attitude that roared at them while its many whiskers writhed in the air as if alive.

The smaller version in her grip twisted, and she let it go. Maybe mommy mutant rat wouldn't hurt them if she got her ugly rat-ling back.

The little monster ran for its parent, and if she'd expected a warm reunion, boy was she fucking wrong.

The baby leaped and grabbed hold of Mama's kicking foot. It clung to it and began to chew. Until Mama stomped down.

Blood and gore spattered. The little monster didn't live to a ripe old mutant age.

Leaving them now with a still super angry mutant rat that turned its baleful gaze on them.

"Shoot it," Peter yelled, brandishing his fancy candle at it.

"With what?"

"What do you mean with what? Don't you have a gun?" He cast her a quick glance.

"Nope. I don't like them."

"Isn't part of your job description bodyguard?"

"I'm more of a hands-on defender."

"Are you fucking serious?"

"Do you have one?" was her sarcastic reply as they both backed away from the monster that had dropped to all four paws.

"Believe when I say I am now regretting not taking the time to find one."

"In the book, didn't the hero dude give it cheese or something?" She grabbed hold of her bag of cheese puffs inside her satchel and waved it. "Here mousy, mousy." She tossed it. "Have some cheese."

For a second the monster eyed it. Then her. Then the cheese puffs again before roaring as it stomped the bag flat.

"Dammit, I was looking forward to those."

"Worry more about the fact it's not happy," he said.

"Ya think?"

"Got a plan?"

"Don't die."

Their grace period was over. The monster was done playing and charged. Peter did the smart human thing and ran. She stood her ground and feinted. She narrowly missed having it take off her head. She ducked and rolled.

Peter yelled, "Hey, ugly fucker, over here."

He'd not gone far. More like flanked the beast. He waved his arms, and she wondered what the hell he was doing other than the obvious—getting himself killed.

"I've got this," she growled, even as she pulled a Matrix, bending over backwards as its prehensile rat-like tail came whipping. The dripping barbs at the end probably wouldn't feel good.

Thunk.

A rock hit the monster in the face. Peter got his death wish. The mutant rodent charged him. And Peter stupidly held his ground.

"You idiot." Then louder, "Here, mousy, mousy. Come to say hello."

But the monster didn't relent, and she fully expected to see Peter gored. Nice knowing you. Sad to see you go.

What a waste of—

For a human, Peter moved faster than expected. One minute he stood there in the path of a gouging horn. The next, he lunged forward and sprang. The man put all kinds of skill into his leap, vaulting nicely in the air, flipping. It was then she realized he still held his can of burning gel. As he rotated over the monster, he spilled it.

Mutant mouse erupted into a torch of living fire.

It squealed and smelled of barbecued meat. The rancid kind that no amount of cooking or spices could fix. It bolted on four legs, aiming for the far side of their dune-covered rocky outcrop. It dove for the sand and began to burrow. The frantic motion extinguished most of the flames. Too late to do it any good. The body stopped twitching.

The night turned still once more. Safe, and her blood was still pumping.

With a smile, she turned to Peter. "So, ready for sex now?"

CHAPTER TWELVE

The crazy thing was that for a second, Peter kind of wanted to say fuck, what just happened, and let's have sex.

His blood ran hot, and his lust even hotter. But... the creature from Hell had left behind a putrid stench. He did his best not to gag in front of Nora. His stomach advised him he might lose that fight.

Sex? Fuck that. He wanted air not stinking of a dead mutant rat. "I don't think now is the right time."

Nora glanced at the body. Its ass end was uncovered, which resulted in ever more noxious gas suddenly billowing.

He moved a few paces downwind from it. She slowly followed.

"Do you not have a sense of smell?" he had to ask.

"I smell incredibly well."

"And don't want to puke?" He wanted to spit and snort the smell out of his lungs and nose.

She shrugged. "Not much bothers me. So you're sure about the sex thing?" She actually waggled her brows and offered a coy smile.

The dead thing audibly farted. Peter was pretty sure he saw green gas and took another step backwards, then two more for good measure.

"You're going in the wrong direction," she said, heading back toward the source of the noxious fumes.

"I'd say you've got that backwards. Why are you getting closer to it?"

"Because it was obviously going somewhere."

"It was burying itself in the ground."

"Not just any part of the ground. It wanted here." She pointed to the section of the dune that had dimpled at the monster's effort. "I wonder if its lair is nearby." She moved close enough to grab a foot and yank.

The body shifted slightly and then dropped suddenly as the spot it was partially buried in caved. The body dangled in her grip. She let it go and teetered on the edge of the newly formed hole.

"Back away!" he yelled.

"I think I see something." She leaned forward.

The ground literally cracked. Fissures appeared,

and the sand shifted, running into the hole like water. Widening its edge. But did Nora step away?

"See you below," she shouted before the ground disappeared and she dropped into the dark maw.

"Nora!" Peter lunged forward even as he knew he couldn't catch her in time. The jagged hole puffed a cloud of dust that blew outward and hid everything in a dirt mist.

Unable to see, he froze. He wouldn't do Nora much good if he fell or got buried too. He mentally ran through his pack of items. Not the most comprehensive thing, given he had to work with what he could buy quickly. But the one thing he did have that didn't take much room? Fishing line that could handle up to three hundred pounds. Enough for him and some leeway to carry something. As he palmed the line, he tried calling out. "Nora? Say something if you can so I know you're alive."

Please don't let her be dead. He'd feel all kinds of bad if she was.

The night remained silent except for the occasional ping of a rock falling. It sounded close. With the dust settled he could once more see the oddly jagged lip of the hole. He noticed no cracking in his section or for a few more feet. He sank to his knees and then his belly, easing forward, pausing to make sure the ground held him.

"Nora."

This time he heard her. "Are you worried about me, Montgomery?" Her tone was light and mocking.

"I wouldn't dare. I take it you're not in imminent danger."

"Not even close. I found something. Our next clue, I think. Come down and see."

"How about you describe it to me as I fashion a harness to pull you up," was his reply as he rolled to this back that he might work the fishing line into something he could use.

"It's a big room. I think it used to have a lot of windows. That's what broke."

A building buried in the sand? Certainly possible. "How many feet down are you?"

"Enough you can hop in. Just don't land hard and you'll be fine."

"I am not joining you."

"Why not?"

"You just saw how unstable it is."

"Because of the windows. They're the weak spots. See." A sudden crack from under him dislodged his precarious perch. He went down, but not as far as expected. He barely remembered to put his hands out in time and protect his face. His palms protested the abuse.

Fuck, *he* protested the abuse. His midsection and

legs hadn't suffered because of a softer landing than expected. He blinked at the dust as it settled. When it did, he saw Nora crouched nearby, holding a torch she'd somehow lit.

"How?"

"I always have a lighter, and gum because some of us had to watch MacGyver growing up." She flicked and a butane flame shot up.

It was then he realized the stick was actually a horn. And the squishy thing he'd landed on? The smell hit him, and his gorge rose. He scrambled off the body.

He ended up in a crouch, arms out as if it would fend off the sky falling. "What the fuck."

"You say that a lot," she remarked.

"It's a good word for when shit is messed up. Like now." He raked fingers through his hair.

"I'm a 'shit' kind of girl. Although I use the occasional fuck."

"Are you seriously discussing swearing with me? We need to get out of here." He raised his gaze to the ragged rim overhead. "It looks like it's only about nine or ten feet to the edge. Maybe if I boost you on my shoulders you can climb out."

"Why would we do that?" she asked, cocking her head, the fire at the tip of her horn illuminating her features.

"To get out of this hole."

"Why? Don't you see? We found the mouse's secret passage to the ice fields."

He glanced around at what appeared to be an old cafeteria. Trestle tables and benches. Counters at the far end. And an angled bank of sand-covered windows that had cracked, dumping a layer into the room.

Doors led off in three directions. The swinging ones at the back reminded him of those in a commercial kitchen.

"How is this supposed to lead us anywhere?"

She pointed past the mound of sand and broken glass that threatened to slice. "If you look over there, you can see where the mouse has traveled."

A line of grime, much of it possibly shit, marked the once light-colored walls.

"You want us to follow that?" He was dubious about the idea. What if there were more mutant mice out there?

"Hell yes I do. By the looks of the signage," she pointed, and he noticed the writing on the wall, "this was some kind of secret operation."

"Doing what?"

"As if I know. Maybe if we check it out, we'll find the next clue."

"There is no way we can make it to any ice fields from here. We're talking miles and miles to the northern edge of the continent. No building is that big."

"You have a better idea?" she asked.

"Finding a way out of this hole," he grumbled.

"Where's your sense of adventure?"

Lost in an old lady's basement. He really needed to man up and get over it. He also didn't need her to point out what a pussy he'd become so he snapped, "How can you be so nonchalant about the fact we're in a hole in the ground?"

"Haven't you ever watched Indiana Jones? This is our temple. Our booby-trapped maze."

Put in those terms, he looked around him with a different eye. The place was well preserved with the glass having lasted until a monster broke it. They could probably search the building quickly and then, when she realized there was nothing to see, they could work on a plan to get out. "Fine. We'll have a look around."

"Sweet," she exclaimed. "Hold on, let me get you a torch too."

He tried to not grimace at the wet ripping sound as she tore the tusk from the beast and handed it to him. She was so unfazed by what she'd done.

As he closed his fingers around it, he couldn't help but ask, "Were you raised in the woods?"

"City actually, but I spent every summer at a ranch."

"And it taught you to use animal horns as torches?"

"Among other things. You coming?" She headed off, maneuvering the collapsed ceiling debris, making her way toward the door to the north.

This was nuts. So unsafe. So stupid to do while sober. "I should have looked harder for some weed," he muttered as he followed.

The door opened with a firm shove and led them to a set of stairs going down into pure darkness but for their torches. They landed in a tunnel that branched in three directions. Nora went straight.

"How do you know where to go?" he asked.

"I'm going north."

The tunnel she chose proved a little disconcerting when they saw the universal symbol for radiation.

Peter cursed as they passed. "Guess that explains the rat. Wonder how much it's leaking? Maybe I'll be lucky and just end up sterile."

"Or you could become a superhero."

The very idea had him snorting. "I am not the type to wear tights. Nor am I some Robin Hood. I steal for me. And only me."

"What about family? Would you steal for them?"

"Of course," he hotly retorted. "Although, it should be noted, my sister would be pissed if she found out. And she's my only family."

"Not anymore. She married, meaning you've just acquired a whole new one."

"Yeah. No thanks. If you'd met her aunts-in-law you'd understand." Lena, Lenore, and Lacey were older women who scared the piss out of him, and he couldn't have said why.

"The triple L's. I've heard of them. And by the sounds of it, they're the equivalent of my sisters. They are always up in my business," Nora huffed. "Because apparently every woman should want to get married and have babies."

"And every guy needs to stop sowing his oats and settle down. I'd rather keep my bachelor pad, hook up when needed, and live my life."

"Exactly!" She eyed him. "With maybe the occasional sleepover."

"For morning sex and breakfast in bed. Most definitely."

"You'd be cooking."

He almost tripped. Surely, he'd misunderstood her implication.

They passed yet another radioactive warning symbol stamped onto a massive metal door, welded shut. He could almost feel it poisoning him.

"Stop flinching every time we walk by one of them."

"Aren't you a little worried we've been exposed?"

"I'm immune."

"No one is immune from radiation," he said.

"I've got really good genes."

"I'm sorry I didn't realize I traveled with a superhero. Must be nice to not worry about getting hurt," was his sarcastic drawled reply.

"Very little can. That's just fact."

Her arrogance had no bounds. "I'm not too proud to admit I have limits."

"You want to go back, go." She pointed. "You'll have to pass all those scary signs again. Me, I'm going forward."

"I'm not a coward." But he did have a strong sense of self-preservation, and he'd pushed it hard enough coming into this hidden underground.

"How did you ever become a thief if you're always worried about risk?"

"A proper theft is the one that isn't noticed. It involves planning and then perfect execution. It doesn't have mutant rats and radiation."

"But on the upside, it has me!" she announced.

"Was that the bonus?"

She pressed against him. "Are you saying I'm not the best prize?"

His hands went to her hips and tugged her close. "I can't think of a better one actually."

"Good answer." She leaned up and kissed him.

He might have enjoyed it more if he wasn't imagining them starting to glow. "Let's find somewhere nicer to finish that."

"This way." She pointed.

"How are you choosing?"

"Well, the next clue was the icy fields. Meaning cold, putting it north of us."

Her simplistic reasoning had him pointing out a flaw in it. "How can you tell where north is?"

"Instinct."

"You mean you're just guessing?"

She laughed. "No, but your reaction was awesome."

"Then how *are* you choosing our route?"

"Mouse tracks."

"We lost those two intersections ago."

"Glad to see you noticed. That's when I switched to following directions. She pointed to the markings at the next intersection. "It's written here."

"You read Russian?"

"No, but I did a summer bootcamp over here and learned some basics."

"What kind of bootcamp?" he asked. Because that sounded kind of fucked up.

"The kind that didn't have flutes or canoes." She winked. "More stairs. How far down does this place go do you think?"

Far enough that even he had to wonder what they'd stumbled upon. A secret installation for hiding nuclear waste?

The stairs were flanked by a ramp layered with rubberized grooves. At the bottom, a forklift, derelict and dusty.

Farther in were more abandoned machines, some of them stripped for parts. Those that acquired them didn't have the same neglected look. They were parked against a wall, clean, looking ready to fire up with a few cranks.

"This doesn't look fully abandoned," Nora stated, eyeing the closed bay doors.

"Was it the working lights that gave it away?" Because it wasn't their torches or windows illuminating the space. He extinguished his tusk.

She glanced overhead at the stringed bulbs. "That explains the humming I've been hearing."

"What humming?" Because he heard nothing.

"Generators running. There are people using this place."

"Are you sure? Because the mouse shit is back." He proudly pointed out the grime he spotted running along the back wall.

"Let's see what's through that curtain." She referred to the strips of plastic hanging down, only partially separating the space.

They entered a loading dock, flanking a rail system that tracked into a wide tunnel.

"Do you think it works?" she asked, eyeing the carts linked together, scuffed and rusted by age.

"Shouldn't the first question be, where does it go?"

She pointed to the markings over the tunnel's opening. "North."

"And of course, you think we should follow."

"Don't you? It's where the mouse is leading us." The shit did indeed seem to border the track and enter the maw of doom.

"Or there are more of them in there, waiting for gullible meat to feed them."

"Don't worry, I'll keep you safe from the mice," she taunted before heading for the carts and peeking inside them. "Empty mostly. But I smell fish?" She sounded confused.

"Fish? Are you sure?" He got close enough that even he caught the faint trace. "Could be illegal fishing being smuggled via that tunnel. It would make sense if this track reaches the sea. Boats could bring in their goods. They bring them in under cover using these carts. Once here, someone trucks them into Siberia, and they're sold on the black market." The presence of the tunnel and carts also explained how the radioactive shit got there, too, without the world noticing it. More than likely the installation used to serve a different purpose before the smugglers took over.

"We found the way to the ice fields," Nora crowed.

"We found something," he corrected even as he questioned his sanity in following the clues in a book written hundreds of years ago. But he'd come too far to give up now.

"I wonder if we can figure out how to get these suckers moving."

Before either of them could search, there was a faraway clanging as of old machinery. Like maybe some bay doors.

Nora stiffened. "Shit. Someone is coming. Hide."

CHAPTER THIRTEEN

As Nora hissed a warning, she pulled Peter by the hand, guiding him past the line of carts to the tunnel of darkness. Not his first choice, but probably their best one. She stubbed out her torch on the way.

They entered the rail tunnel and flattened themselves against the wall. He heard the rustle of plastic and the rapid-fire speech of two people, a man and woman by the sounds of it. One of them whistled as if for a dog. More talk then the rumble of an engine that turned into a scream of metal as the gears for the track started to chug.

"What do you say we catch a ride?" Nora whispered as she tugged him farther into the tunnel, well out of sight of anyone watching. The carts, still gaining speed, trundled past, and she threw herself into one.

He jumped into the next and gripped the edge of it. He could see nothing.

"Why are you all the way over there? Hold on, I'm coming."

"Wait? What?" He might have said more, but he could hear her climbing from her cart to his. "Be careful," he exclaimed just as she landed.

"Please, I've done that with roller coasters going full tilt. I can handle this kiddy ride."

"You think we should stay on it? We don't even know where it goes."

"Guess we'll find out. In the meantime, let's get comfy." She tugged him down beside her. He shifted his pack off his back. Given the chill, he grabbed his thin but thermal-rated blanket. He leaned to spread it over her and felt her warm chuckle.

"I'm not cold."

Indeed, she radiated heat. "I'm chilly so humor me and share."

"You need me to heat you up?" she teased. It didn't matter he couldn't see her in the dark. He could practically see her smile.

"Not sure now is the time."

"Why not?"

He could have given a list of reasons. But that wouldn't give him what he wanted.

Her.

He twisted and felt for her in the dark, his hand finding and cupping her jaw to draw her to him.

They kissed, a soft press of lips that turned passionate. Her mouth clung to his, open and inviting. His tongue said hello. His hands roamed all over her body.

They were in the most awkward place, and yet it didn't matter. She ended up in his lap, straddling his thighs, hands cupping his face. She licked the seam of his lips, nibbling on him, making noises to drive him wild.

His hands palmed her ass, squeezing it through the athletic material of her leggings. He was so fucking hard he thought he might burst out of his pants.

"I wanna lick you again," he groaned.

"I think that sounds like a fine plan. Scooch down a little and use your pack as a pillow," she suggested as the rustle of fabric indicated clothes coming off.

He scooched and had to bend his knees since his feet hit the far end of the cart. He was at an angle and the perfect height, as it turned out. While still kneeling, she thrust her mound against his face.

"Lick me," she ordered.

He obeyed, spreading her plump lips with his tongue, tasting the sweetness that was all her. Salty, too, to give it a hint more depth. She rose over his face and mouth, moaning as he brought her to the edge. He maneuvered a hand close enough he could thrust a finger inside her.

She clamped down hard on it and whimpered. "Fuck me."

He wanted nothing more. "Sit on my cock."

Her turn to obey as she practically tore open his pants to get at his dick. Her eager hands grabbed him, and he grunted, hips thrusting into her grip.

"Look at you, big boy. This is gonna be fun." She pressed the tip of him against her, and he managed to gasp.

"Condom!" He had some. Somewhere. Fuck, he was so close.

"Don't worry about that. I've got us covered."

She sat down hard on him. He almost exploded. The intense fisting of her pussy around him had him sucking in for air, his body rigid. And when she started to move, he couldn't help but dig his fingers into her hips.

She knew how to grind against him and give his cock that tight, loving care it craved. She flexed her muscles and stroked him so hard he soon gasped, "Can't hold on. Can't."

As if his words were a trigger, she came. Hard. Tight. Flexing his cock. Milking his orgasm and drawing it out until he almost screamed with the intensity of it.

She collapsed on him.

They both panted.

It was so fucking incredible. Mind blowing. So when she said, "Wanna do it again?"

His very coherent reply? "Un-hunh."

CHAPTER FOURTEEN

Time passed slowly and too quickly in that dark den where they explored each other's bodies by touch and taste alone.

Peter's stamina didn't quite match hers but proved impressive for a human. As a lover, he satisfied her more than she could have imagined. If she had to resign herself to three times a day, then so be it.

He dozed in the bottom of the cart, his body curled around hers. Dressed because danger wouldn't wait for them to put on garments. Or so he claimed.

Nora had a feeling it had more to do with the fact he felt the deepening chill as they reached their destination. To her, it was still comfortable. The difference in what they could handle was more than she wanted to examine. She had to treat his delicate constitution more carefully than she would her own.

He'd flip if she ever said that to him, though. He had pride. Even if she explained her differences, she had to wonder if he'd still be so accepting of her. Right now, he didn't seem to mind her expertise, but what if she continued to surpass him?

Not all men could handle it. Was it wrong she'd hoped for someone who could handle her?

She woke him as the tunnel finally began to lighten. "Come on. This is where we get off," she whispered.

He didn't say a word but gathered his bag and blanket and, as the cart slowed, followed her over the edge before they could be spotted by someone waiting at the end of the track. They inched along the tunnel, crouching as they neared the entrance, and the voices.

More Russians, yelling, talking, doing all kinds of loud shit while they waited. And waited.

In the movies, everything seemed to happen quickly. The reality involved a lot of patience. Eventually the carts went chugging back up the tunnel, heavily laden with fish and other aquatic delicacies: lobsters, crab, even some seal. The smell made her hungry. She really regretted giving up her cheese puffs. She could have popped them into her mouth and sucked them until she could swallow without a crunch. Taste that salty goodness.

She was head back, almost moaning, when he

whispered in her ear. "You better be thinking of me." His arm came around her, and his hand slid between her legs. Rubbed against her and she writhed against his hand.

Wrong time and he knew it. He was teasing her on purpose. He fired her blood and made her hungry.

The carts had clacked out of sight, and so she had to bite her tongue as he slid a hand inside her leggings. He stroked her, fingered her clit in a way that had her rocking against his hand. When she turned, it was to kiss him, and keep kissing him as he finger-fucked her, making her come on his hand. She clutched him and force herself to hold back lest she hurt him. She stifled it and almost passed out from the exertion. When it was done, she leaned her forehead against his while he stroked her back.

She'd managed to once more hold back instead of letting go and getting too rough with him. But how long would she be able to keep doing that before she forgot and lost control?

His fingers pulled away, and she focused back on the present with its fading voices as the people left with a clang of metal as of doors closing. The mouth of the tunnel grew quiet. She waited a bit longer before slipping to the entrance and peering out. Unlike the platform where they left, they'd arrived in a massive ice cavern with a watery slip sloshing waves onto a dock covered in ice. The water didn't look warm.

In the corner of the cave sat a few large metal containers, interlocked with tunnels. From the roof of one, smoke emerged. Not everyone had left, and she didn't see any icy fields. "I think we'll have to get out of the cave if we want to see anything."

Exiting meant exposing their presence to the container habitats. Only two of them had windows. Two too many if anyone watched.

No one raised an alarm, and soon they were maneuvering the slick rocks at the mouth of the cavern. The water had formed a layer of ice that sent a deep chill through the skin.

Once past the first few feet, it got easy to climb. Not that she had any issues, and neither did Peter. He kept showing a surprising resiliency. He'd be formidable if he had even half the gifts being a shifter gave her.

The entire climb, he wore a grim expression. So sexy. Pity he'd probably balk at a quickie while halfway up their climb.

When they reached the top, he paused, hands on his thighs, breathing heavy. Whereas she hadn't even broken a sweat.

She did squint, though. "Wow is it bright." A sheet

of white glinted as far as the eye could see, refracting and bathing the world in the purest of light.

"A diamond field. Just like the story." He shook his head.

"Are you starting to believe in our quest?" she asked.

"I will admit it's been pretty fucking wild so far. And all because of you. You've got a really good sixth sense for this stuff."

More like a good nose and a heavy dose of curiosity. Already this mission had born fruit. Arik would want to know about the illegal fishermen. The preservation of denizens of the sea was of high importance to cats. They loved their surf and turf.

"In the book, he emerged at noon and the world was blinding," she said, pivoting to look around. "But he could see one thing." She pointed.

"The edge of the world," he stated. "Looks like the ice ends in a cloud."

They headed for it, moving as quickly as they could on foot. She knew he had to be cold, and yet he didn't complain. Just marched with determination.

Still, she couldn't help but worry. Frostbite was a very real threat to him, as was hypothermia. Shifters ran hotter and weren't as affected.

At least they didn't have too far to go. The clouds

got closer, and as they did, she said, "The air is getting warmer."

"I think we found the volcano," was his reply.

Soon enough, the humid mist enveloped them, and she caught Peter by the arm before he stepped off the edge.

"You might want to find a path that doesn't result in you diving to your death," she suggested.

He knelt and glanced down, muttering, "There has to be a path." He was the one to find a ledge leading down and then into the volcano and curving and swirling, bringing them lower. He held her hand, and his excitement hummed through her.

They were almost there. At the end of the tunnel, they'd find the treasure.

Oh, and one last thing.

An abominable monster.

CHAPTER FIFTEEN

"Oh my God!" Peter exclaimed.

"Ditto," Nora squealed. "Isn't it just the cutest!" She clapped her hands in glee.

The Russian yeti rose in a shaggy ball of white-gray fur. It flashed an impressive array of teeth, thrust its horns, and uttered a big, "*Grawr.*"

"I want it!" Nora exclaimed. She would hug it and love it and call it Fluffy.

"You do realize that thing is eyeing us as its next dinner," he declared.

Indeed, it waved its paws and did its best to appear fearsome. "It's so fluffy!" She had two weaknesses. Sherpa sweaters and big cuddly yetis. She'd even gone to the Rockies a half-dozen times in the hopes of finding one. At last, her dream was coming true. "You'll be my best friend." She threw herself at the yeti, only to miss.

She missed! It was so rare that she lay there stunned for a second before she looked up, and up some more, past the fluted foot of a pedestal.

"I found it!" she squealed. In her excitement over the stuffed toy come to life, she'd almost forgotten the real reason for being here.

She sprang to her feet and glanced over the ornate box inlaid with bright metal but, oddly enough, showing no slot for a key. Which might explain the pile she spotted past the pedestal. All kinds of keys in a heap mixed with bones. Lots of bones. They were not the first ones to come here.

"I think the treasure might be cursed," she told him.

"Well, duh. Big monster guarding it," Peter said as he slid his bag from his back.

"Hardly a monster. Fluffy is the cutest thing I've ever seen." Nora smiled as she whirled and caught her soon-to-be pet trying to give her a hug. "Come here, cutie." She reached out and snared its arms and dragged it close.

"Are you hugging that monster?"

"It's adorable. I'm gonna keep it."

"You cannot keep it. You don't even know what it is."

"Russian yeti."

"I don't think there's any such thing as a Russian yeti."

"Then what would you call my new friend?" She gave it a shake. Fluffy squeaked.

"Not a friend for starters," Peter huffed, edging sideways. He had his tiny little knife in hand.

"Don't you dare poke my Fluffy." She shoved the yeti behind her and huffed. Hot misty air in. Tangy. And smelling burnt. Odd how it wasn't hotter, though. The arctic sea and ice must be keeping the temperature down.

"Are you trying to get eaten?" he declared, waving the knife.

"She's not going to hurt us. Are you, Fluffy?" She whirled toward the yeti, who backed away, head cocked, watching them both warily.

"She doesn't understand you."

"I disagree. She is totally listening to us."

"Grawr," Fluffy replied in the affirmative.

Whereas Peter frowned. "It does seem more docile than expected."

"She."

"How can you tell?"

"How can you not?" Nora repeated mockingly. "Although I am flattered your head isn't turned by just any lady in fur."

"I don't believe in fur, although I do like steak."

"Depends on the fur. If I was wearing it, you'd stroke it."

Something gagged. Her poor Fluffy obviously had a hairball.

"I can't believe we found the place in the book." Peter spun around, slowly taking in the massive cavern covered in a sheet of ice as heat from the fissures in the ground froze. A heavy mist hung a few feet over their heads. A few openings led off the room, and it was tempting to check them out. After.

First, she had a box to open.

Fluffy stood in front of the pedestal.

"Move, Fluffy. I'm here for the treasure."

Her new pet bared her teeth.

"Now, now, is that any way to talk to me? And to think, I was gonna find us some meat for dinner tonight."

Fluffy gagged again.

Wait. Was her new pet a vegetarian? Or more horrifying, "Are you a vegan?"

Fluffy shook her head.

She sighed in relief. "But you're trying to tell me something. I'm going to go on a limb and say, stay away from the box."

Fluffy went wild bobbing.

Even Peter took notice.

"Is it because there's a curse?" Because all fairy tales had one.

More frantic bobbing that led to Peter mocking. "It is becoming obvious you've watched too many movies featuring animals as people. That thing is most definitely not trying to tell us anything other than we look tasty."

"You can be really close minded, you know."

"Being strait-laced is what got me out of the hospital," he muttered.

"The world is full of things that seem inexplicable," she said, her attention drawn by a noise.

Fluffy's head angled as well. It appeared they had company.

"Science will eventually explain everything." Peter, with his human ears, hadn't noticed.

"No it won't." Her firm belief.

He finally heard the approaching herd of humans, their attempts to be stealthy far from subtle. "Someone's coming."

"I'm hoping it's the guys who stole the key." It would be kind of them to deliver themselves into her paws.

Five men ran into the room—because their females were obviously too smart to tangle with Nora. They were armed with regular guns, not tranquilizing darts.

That didn't stop her new pet from trying to protect them.

Fluffy uttered a roar and waved her arms as she ran for them, only to get shot.

"Fluffy! No!" Nora yelled as her new best friend hit the ground and rolled into a crack hissing with steam.

Nora snarled as she faced the humans. "I will tear off your face and eat it," she yelled. Only to realize a second later she couldn't keep her promise. Unless she planned to kill Peter too. He'd probably notice if she turned feline and started chewing on people.

She had to settle for running at the humans. A bullet grazed her shoulder. Not incapacitating, but since they might get luckier than a Stormtrooper and manage a headshot, she pretended to go down.

Peter didn't like that. "You mother fuckers. You shot her."

"We'll shoot you, too, if you don't get out of the way," the leader of the group boldly stated as he sauntered forward.

The thud of a fist hitting flesh resulted in a howl of pain and a guy shouting, "Want me to shoot him?" Him being Peter, who'd slugged the leader of the humans.

She'd have to protect him. She dug her fingers into the ground and prepared to spring.

"Not yet," said the fellow rubbing his jaw. He smirked as he pulled out the key and waved it. "I say we let him see what's in the box then kill him so his ghost can have all kinds of regret."

It was the stupidest thing she'd ever heard, and yet the fellow seemed so pleased with himself. Smug fucker. As he strutted past her, she coiled herself, ready to pounce, only to freeze as a new player joined them.

A woman with russet hair entered the cave, and before anyone could react, she shot two of the humans, aimed at a third, and said, "Put down your guns. Or you all die."

Everyone listened.

Heck, Nora kind of wanted a gun to toss down in homage. That was some fine shooting and threats.

Rising to her feet, tickled by a sense she should recognize the girl, Nora readied to confront her. Only she was ignored as the newcomer focused on Peter and said, "I am Svetlana Koznetsov! You killed my grandmother. Prepare to die."

CHAPTER SIXTEEN

Shades of *Princess Bride* made the woman's declaration strange. Things got crazier as a tiger stepped out from the tunnel.

It was his red balloon moment.

The one that woke him in a sweat at night.

That made him wish he had a gun.

The evil tiger that haunted him rubbed against the granddaughter of Irina Koznetsov.

"I didn't kill Irina." Peter pointed. "That did."

"Grandmother's tiger would have never eaten her. She's owned it her whole life," Svetlana declared, petting the feline head, obviously not taking note of the glare it shot her way. "It used to babysit me when Grandma had her afternoon naps."

"Your grandma's tiger has a taste for human flesh. Trust me, I know."

"It's a meat eater. It's in its nature," defended the stupid girl.

"How long have you been following me?" he snapped.

"Since you resurfaced a few weeks ago. Although I've been looking since you killed my grandmother and stole the key." Svetlana kept her weapon steady as she headed for the guy with the key.

One of the attackers moved. Without turning her head, Svetlana shot him in the leg, and he'd have sworn he heard Nora mutter, "Nice."

"What do you know about the key?" he asked.

"That it's important. I can't believe as a child I used it to make that stupid junky light for my grandma. When I showed a picture of it to a friend of mine who studies ancient legends, he just about lost his mind because it was identical to a key in some story he did a dissertation on. Imagine my surprise when I came for a visit to see my grandmother and the damned thing was gone. Stolen. And I found poor kitty locked in a cage with Grandma's shredded clothing."

"Proving the cat killed her."

"Because you gave it no choice, locking them in together."

He didn't know how to argue with someone this irrational. "I knew I shouldn't have come back to Russia." All his problems stemmed from here.

"Hand it over." Having reached the leader of the goons who'd stolen the key, Svetlana held out her palm. The guy hesitated only a second in front of the gun pointed at his face. Her fingers curled around the key. "Now to see what all the fuss is about."

"Grawr." The tiger apparently had issues with the plan.

"Don't get pissy with me, kitty. I brought you along to teach him a lesson. So get on with it," Svetlana snapped.

As if it could understand, the tiger stepped toward him, but he held his ground. Running would just make it easier for the animal to take him down. Then again, he didn't put his chances high in hand-to-claw battle either.

Nora stepped between them.

The tiger snarled.

And Nora...

Well, Nora snarled back.

He recoiled in surprise. It was rather realistic as cat sounds went.

The tiger paused before sidling as if to go around her.

"You really don't want to do that," Nora said in a soft threat.

"I'd listen to Nora if I were you," announced Zach as he suddenly stepped into the cave, hands held out as if unarmed. For a place that had supposedly been hidden for a long freaking time, it appeared to have a lot of visitors.

"Who the hell are you?" Svetlana asked, clutching the key while pointing her gun.

"The guy who hates the cold and yet happens to be in Russia, inside a volcano in the middle of a big-ass freezing tundra. Now, are you going to put down your gun, or should I just assume I'll have to kill you?"

That was harsh even by Peter's standards, and this guy was usually Nora's partner. It only reinforced his belief that Nora must work for the mob.

Svetlana looked as if she'd argue.

Zach shrugged. "Have it your way then."

"I will!" Svetlana fired, but Zach was already moving, slipping into a thickening mist rising from the vents in the floor.

It was then Nora acted, whirling, her foot arcing and connecting, knocking the gun out of Svetlana's hand then grabbing the Russian girl by the wrist and twisting. Svetlana cried out.

"Give me the key."

"It's not yours," Svetlana snarled a second before all hell broke loose.

Fluffy suddenly popped into view and dove on one of the original goons. Goon number two started firing. Peter heard a roar as the tiger threw itself at him.

Everything got fast and slow and blurry and too big at the same time.

Flying fur. Shouts. Gunshots. Snarls.

And that was when it happened. Peter began hallucinating again, but this time, instead of thinking he saw a tiger shifting into an old woman, he saw his lover turned into a lion. He blinked, and it just happened. Human one minute, big golden feline the next. The lion slammed into the tiger. They went down in a spitting, heaving mass of fur.

Then his psychotic break went even deeper as Zach appeared from the mist, a big, naked man who turned into a lion with a bushy dark mane.

But the shock of his mind making him think that people around him were turning into animals wasn't what took him to his knees. For that, blame the bullet.

CHAPTER SEVENTEEN

The fight itself didn't take long, but by the time it was done, more than a few had died. All the goons for one. Zach was already at work, shoving at the bodies with his snout and paws, ridding them in the deep vents lining the volcano basin.

The tiger lay on the ground panting, not so much injured as old and tired. Nora wasn't out to kill the old lady, despite the things she'd done. After all, she used to have a grandmother that thought milking virgin goats by mouth would get rid of wrinkles. Sometimes old people did things the old ways. It was up to the next generations to teach them.

"It's over, Irina," she declared.

The tiger sighed and shifted, fur turning to flesh.

Svetlana gasped. "Grandmother? Is that you?"

How could the girl not know her roots? Would they have to bury another body?

Speaking of which. The tang of blood permeated the air, and it took her a moment to realize some of it came from behind her.

Peter.

A whirl and she was on him, pressing her fingers to the bullet wound, trying to stem the flow of blood.

"We need to stop this." She needed to keep applying pressure.

"Wishing you the best with that. In case you hadn't noticed, my luck is shit." He coughed and convulsed a little, making the hot liquid gush.

Panic, rare and unwelcome, made her mouth sour. "Maybe if I cauterize it."

"Don't you dare brand me with that mutant horn." He closed his eyes and gasped for air.

"I have to do something." Anything. She couldn't just let him die.

"Show me the treasure." She almost didn't hear his whisper.

"You can't be serious."

"If I'm gonna die, I wanna see why. What's in the box?"

"You aren't dying," she groused. Still she yelled for Zach. "I need the key."

The lion bobbed his mane and stalked for Svetlana, who clutched it to her chest.

Irina cuffed her. "Let him have it. He'll tear off your head before you can kill him."

The woman gritted her teeth as Zach stalked over, lithe in his movements as he went from lion to man. A very big and naked man.

"Hand it over," Zach demanded.

Svetlana didn't argue. She dropped it into his palm.

Zach carried it to Nora, who explained, "Peter wants to see what's in the box before he gets a few stitches."

"I heard. I'll bring him."

"Like fuck is a naked dude carrying me." Peter gave Zach a side eye that made him laugh.

"Don't flatter yourself. I'm into tits and fur, little man."

If the situation weren't dire, she would have laughed. "Let Zach carry you, or you won't see the treasure."

"Is that any way to talk to a dying man? Wait, wouldn't want to complain. You might actually try and play the violin." Peter's wan joke almost earned him a slap.

This time he didn't exaggerate. Stupid fragile human.

They gathered around the pillar where the box

appeared welded in place to the stone. It was cold compared to the heat within the basin. Icy cold when she ran her hand over it. It seemed so weird given the cavern was rather warm.

"I don't know where to insert the key." Nora didn't see a spot. Her gaze flitted to the pile behind and the bleached skulls.

"Maybe it's invisible," Peter said. He was being held upright by Zach. His eyes half shut.

"That's dumb," she stated, jabbing the key at the box, only to freeze as it went in. "Holy shit. I found a hole." She shoved it until it would go no more. She then grabbed his limp hand.

"Let's do this together," she said before she held him tight and turned the key.

It stuck partway. Wouldn't turn, so she shoved harder and it snapped.

Her horror emerged in a vehement, "Mother fucker!"

Peter chuckled. "Guess I won't be seeing inside it. Just my luck."

Fatalistic and she was suddenly ready to cry. She slammed her fists onto the closed box, yelling, "Open up, damn you."

To her surprise, and probably everyone else's, it did.

"What's in it?" Peter asked.

She leaned to look in because she couldn't see anything other than a pool of darkness. She put her face right into the opening and got downright chilly, as if fingers strummed her inner essence. She sucked in a surprised breath. Cold, so cold, and now inside her.

She retreated, her breath frosting.

"Well?" asked Peter. "Did you find treasure?"

She rubbed her knuckles over his cheek. "I did. Not the kind I ever imagined, though."

He closed his eyes. "Me too. Nora."

If only they'd had more time. If he'd been a bit sturdier. How she wished he were a shifter like her. Then a simple bullet wound would have just been a temporary irritation. If only she could have one more chance.

Her lips touched his, and her breath suddenly expelled in a cold rush.

Peter's body jerked. His eyes opened, but he didn't see her, she'd wager, given the shiny film that slid over them.

He began to shake and shiver, the motion fast enough to make him blurry. She rocked away from him as his form wavered and shook, changed shape. Grew fur.

What the fuck?

Zach inched farther away, but she got closer.

Could it be possible? That cold breath she'd sucked

in from the box and expelled on Peter, was it magic? In the book, it didn't say what the hero and tsarina found. Only that they were granted their wish.

Her wish. For them to be together.

And that resulted in a very freaked-out lion.

CHAPTER EIGHTEEN

Peter opened his mouth to yell because, fucking shit, his body had just gone through the most traumatizing pain. Only it emerged as a roar.

Uh. What?

"Roar."

He kept doing it. Every time he opened his mouth.

"Roar."

"Roar."

Fuck. No, it still came out as a roar. No!

The panic was real as he ran, pushing past the interesting-smelling people. The big guy had a bit of a hot spice and musky thing going. Nora was all sweetness and almost enough to distract him from his sprint. However, the full-blown panic was in effect.

He'd completely lost his mind. He thought he was a lion. He'd be locked in the loony bin forever.

Before he could make it far, a body tackled him. A golden-furred body that pinned him to the floor. He might have fought except he knew that scent.

Nora. Wait, how could he know her by smell? And why was it giving him a boner? Oh fuck. How could he be thinking of sex when he'd gone insane?

Woe is me. He went limp. Might as well wait for the men in the white coats.

A nose nudged him. A moment later Nora crooned to him, "Come on, you big pussy cat. Stop freaking out. Calm down. It's not a big deal."

Not a big deal? He thought he was a lion.

He didn't want to be a lion.

And suddenly he wasn't. It didn't help. Because now he was naked, sitting on the pebbled ground. "Those doctors are right. I am crazy," he muttered.

"Not crazy," a very naked Nora argued.

Was he imagining that too? "I thought I was shot. But look at me, I'm not hurt. I saw you open the box, only it was empty. And then I thought I was a pussycat. Then you were a giant cat. Maybe it's the gasses making me hallucinate."

"That all happened, Peter. Every bit of it," she said softly.

"But..."

"No buts. Shifters are real."

"Real?" He glanced at his hands. It sounded impossible. Yet a moment ago they'd been covered in fur. "How?"

She shrugged. "Maybe one day they'll have a scientific explanation, but for the moment, magic suffices. And before you ask, unlike you, I was born this way."

"Born a lion?"

"Born a shifter. Skinwalker. Whatever you want to call it. And now, so are you."

"I'm a lion." Saying it didn't make it feel real.

What did was an inner rumbling, an instinct that yelled, *Danger.*

His ears pricked, his attention too. Nora's head lifted, and she turned, alert. "We need to get out of here. The volcano sounds like it's waking up."

Saying it pretty much triggered the tremor. The world shook, and suddenly the steam and heat in the room rose a few degrees.

Zach yelled, "We need to get out of here."

"Not without Fluffy."

"We don't have time to go looking for it."

"Where's the box?" Nora asked with a glance at the pedestal. Bare. Box and key gone. Irina and Svetlana too. Cracks began forming in the floor.

"Let's get out of here." Peter grabbed Nora's hand and went to run, only a fissure erupted, splitting their path.

Zach didn't hesitate. He turned into a lion and soared.

Nora released his hand. "Shift, run, and jump."

"I—" He was going to say can't.

But if he didn't, he'd die.

Nora smiled at him. "You've got this. You're one of us now. Do you know what that means?" She leaned close to whisper by his ear. "We won't be limited to three times."

He hardened as she whirled and bolted, changing as she ran until she was a golden, sleek feline soaring over the crack. Then it was his turn.

His turn to become the impossible.

Go, go, lion body.

He waited.

Nothing. The rumbling deepened, and the steam jetted hot enough to curl hair. Now or never. He just started running, while praying.

If I am a lion, then let's hear me roar.

More like a strangled *grawr*, but he, too, made the impossible leap to the other side. Landing on four feet, he joined the other cats.

Casting a glance over his shoulder, he caught a glimpse of the pedestal a moment before it exploded into blue lava. Blue was hotter than red if he remembered correctly.

Time to really go.

They raced up the tunnel to the edge of the volcano and then kept running. His four-legged body more comfortable the longer he wore it.

Liberating as well. Strong. Without tiring as expected, he managed to run all the way to the helicopter Zach had flown in. They lifted off and not a second too soon, as the plateau it was parked on cracked and lava boiled its way through.

The good news was Peter wasn't being roasted in it. His luck had finally changed. He was alive, in one piece, and with an incredible woman that he was pretty sure he loved.

He laced his fingers with hers, and she turned to smile at him before laying her head on his shoulder. The true treasure, by his side.

That night, in their hotel bed, he worshipped every inch of her. Kissed her from those succulent lips to the backs of her knees. He drew the line at toes. He licked her until she came bucking against his face.

He teased her nipples until she humped his thigh so vigorously he worried about chafing.

He then fucked her. On her back. Knees. Sideways. In the shower. Bouncing her as he walked her back to bed for more fucking.

And even after all that sex, he wanted her even more.

Which was why, during their flight home to America, right after a quickie in the bathroom on the airplane, he said, "I love you."

"So do I," she said with a kiss. And followed with, "Just do me a favor and don't ever tell my sisters."

"Why?"

"Because if they know you love me and that I love you, then next thing you know they'll have talked you into jerking off into a cup so they can check the motility of your sperm."

"But I don't want kids," was his dumb reply.

She patted his cheek. "Me neither. But that won't stop them from trying. So avoid the oysters at Christmas. They like to lace them with Viagra to give the great-uncles a cheap thrill and piss off the aunts."

"Are they lions like you?"

She laughed. "No one is like me."

And that was the lion's honest truth.

Rawr.

EPILOGUE

Back in the States, explaining all she had seen proved interesting. Some folks leaned on the skeptical side and assumed the incident in the volcano had triggered a latent gene in Peter. Others pondered the what-if aspect of the strange magic in the box that had escaped into the big wild world.

Given they wanted to find it, Nora's new assignment was to try and track down where Irina and her granddaughter went. Most of all, find the box.

The mission came with a new partner. But that wasn't the reason Peter spent more time in her condo than at his place. Not that she minded. Waking up snuggled together was fast becoming her favorite new thing.

Working with Peter was much different than with

Zachary. For instance, she'd never had to balance doing her job in between so much sex. Good thing they could be quick when needed, saving the longer sessions for when they went to bed.

He met her family, and when his sisters started in on him about his potential as a sperm donor, he went into a sad diatribe about his compromised mutant sperm. Then said how perfect Nora was for him because she had mutant eggs from that same radioactive incident.

She wasn't sure her sisters believed it, but she found it amusing to watch him try.

Despite all the change, Peter appeared to have adjusted to his new normal. But the Pride was still spinning with the knowledge that there was a game-changer out in the world, possibly in the wrong hands.

Had the discovery of the box ushered in the end of everything they knew?

Or was this a new beginning?

She had to wonder as she writhed in a patch of sunlight, golden fur soaking in those hot rays until something bulky caused a shadow. She opened one lazy eye to her mate standing there, majestic as fuck with his wildly long mane. Thankfully Peter was not interested in trying to rule and ripping their pride apart.

He shifted, his long, lean body showing fewer signs of the scars. His hair was thicker. His skin clearer. As if he'd shed the unhealthy and found himself renewed.

It had an effect on his vigor. Now she was the one scrambling to keep up when he gave her that grin.

"We've got a few minutes before we need to dress and leave for the party." He arched a brow in invitation.

She stretched and loved how his gaze smoldered as it eyed her. "So I heard something interesting today from the team studying those fairy tale books."

"Oh?" he said, dropping to a knee and lifting her leg over his shoulder to expose her.

"I found out the name of the hero," she said. And the reason why he wouldn't tell her what it was.

She screamed it when he made her come. "Peter." The hero who got the happily ever after, the key needed to unlock her lion heart.

BEFORE NORA and Peter joined the mile-high club but after the volcano erupted...

The entire flight back to the airport where he'd borrowed the chopper from, Zach didn't let on that he knew about the stowaway. Nor did he worry too much about them. He could smell the fear of whatever hid behind the storage area where he'd tossed some equipment aboard in case things went sideways in the arctic.

Nora and her transformed human only had eyes for each other. The hormones rolling off them were distracting. To dump them quickly, he told them to take his rental. He'd catch a ride in a taxi.

As the newly infatuated couple went off, he pretended to check over the chopper, waiting until they were out of sight to say, "You can come out now."

His curiosity had him sniffing and trying to figure out who'd snuck aboard. He didn't know the scent and wasn't sure what to expect other than he knew it wasn't Svetlana or her grandmother. Nor was his stowaway human. He just couldn't have said what she was. "I know you're in there. Come out."

The rustling preceded the biggest fucking eyes, a bright and icy blue. Fine features framed by silver and gray hair that hung down over her naked frame. The female blinked thick lashes at him. Her lip sucked in as if she were nervous.

"Who the fuck are you?" he barked, not at all taken in by her innocent face.

Only to blink at her unexpected reply. "Fluffy."

GRUFF AND TOUGH ZACH ISN'T ONE TO FALL FOR A PRETTY FACE, BUT THERE'S MORE TO FLUFFY

ALEENA THAN MEETS THE EYE, WHICH MIGHT MAKE HER PERFECT FOR A Lion's Mate.

More books in A Lion's Pride:

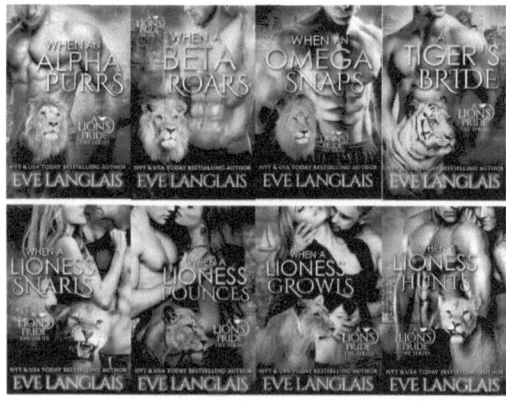

Need some new shifters to love?

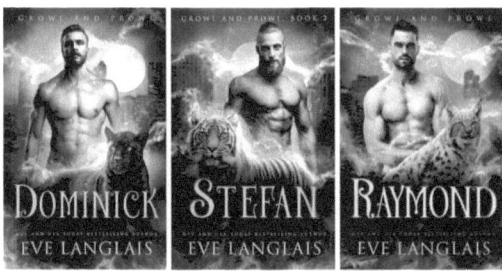

Be sure to visit www.EveLanglais for more books with furry heroes, or sign up for the Eve Langlais newsletter for notification about new stories or specials.

www.ingramcontent.com/pod-product-compliance
Lightning Source LLC
LaVergne TN
LVHW041635060526
838200LV00040B/1575